FLOWERS IN DECEMBER

BOOKS BY JANE SUEN

Children of the Future
Flowers in December

FLOWERS IN DECEMBER

Jane Suen

FLOWERS IN DECEMBER
Copyright © 2016 by Jane Suen

This book is a work of fiction. Names, characters, places, and incidents are products of the author's imagination or are used fictitiously. Any resemblance to actual persons, living or dead, events, or locales is coincidental.

Jane Suen's books are available for order through Ingram Press Catalogues

www.janesuen.com

Printed in the United States of America

First Printing: November 2016

ISBN: 978-0-9979297-2-0
Ebook ISBN: 978-0-9979297-3-7

In loving memory of my grandmother
and
Amei and Kiti, my beloved orange tabby cats

Chapter 1

Connor closed the door behind him. He had been dreading this moment. He stood, immobilized. He saw her coffin…across the room, yet he couldn't move. After a long time, he finally took his first step. Reaching her open casket, his throat tightened as he gazed upon her face. He searched, in vain, for familiarity and warmth, but he found only the harshness of rigidity and coldness. His eyes misted, blurring his view. He stepped back as tears welled up and streamed down his face. A droplet fell, and then another as his tears turned into a torrent. No longer caring who would hear him, he released his sobs and wailed into the silent walls as if they could comfort him.

Connor knelt in front of the coffin and whispered her name. First he spoke softly and gently, between sobs racked with pain. Then he shouted her name, over and over, as if he could bring her back. He lost track of the time. Eventually, his sobs subsided.

Chapter 2

Connor lay crumpled next to her coffin, not willing to get up just yet, not ready to leave. He let his mind wander, thinking about his mother, himself as a little boy. This was the one time, the one trip Connor had never wanted to take.

It was a long drive across the state—he had traveled for miles and miles without seeing a gas station, without seeing a mile marker. As the city faded behind him and he drove further and further away, Connor felt a new sense of freedom. He opened his sunroof, basked in the warm rays of the sun, felt the rush of the wind, smelled the fresh air, and tuned into nature. His worries and burdens were swept away with the wind. The further away he got from the city, the better he felt. The vastness of this land, the beauty of it, stirred something deep inside of him. He had escaped the four solid walls of his office with his coveted window, the office he had worked so hard to attain…and that he was now imprisoned in. Long hours, day after day, with little time for fun.

When Connor had first received the call about his mother, he felt a twinge of guilt, knowing that he hadn't visited as often as he should have. Her death was sudden and unexpected. The last time he went home was over the holidays, last year. His family was small, just the three of them: him, his mom and dad. He didn't have kids, wasn't married. His parents had long stopped asking that question. His father had passed first. Now it was his mother. He was the only one left.

Images from long ago appeared, unbidden yet not unwelcome. The time she had surprised him with a birthday party and a pony ride. He had pestered her for this, but she had been cautious. He wanted what every little boy wanted, and he thought that a pony ride was just the thing. As a little boy, he had been fearless; he did crazy things just to see if he could. "Do first and ask later" was his motto. When his parents had found out, he got plenty of whippings for his mischief. He had grown up in the small town. He knew his parents were disappointed that he didn't stay, that he left like so many of the kids before him, packing up his bags as soon as he graduated high school and heading to the big, shining city. He got a little scholarship at the community college and worked hard to get established with solid academics. After two years, he transferred to the state college.

Connor had immersed himself in his studies. The thought of crawling back to his hometown and admitting failure drove him harder each time things got tough. During a particularly rough semester, he seriously thought about throwing in the towel—he even told himself he was meant to live out his life in the little town of Rocky Flats, doing what every generation of the Nortons had done. Maybe he was meant to inherit his family's little hardware store and live out his life there.

No! He was determined to get away.

Now, twenty years later, he was going home at age thirty-eight. He had achieved success and climbed the corporate ladder.

He remembered his mom on his last visit, straightening his shirt collar. "Connor, you know you have more clothes at home. You can come and get them anytime."

"Mom…I know you want me to wear them, but they are out of style. I have to buy new shirts and suits every year." He paused. "I rotate my shirts and suits and take them to the donation center. I have to dress a certain way."

"The styles will come back. They always do, you know."

"Yes, Mom. I know."

"You're my pride and joy, always remember this." She kissed him on the cheek and tugged lovingly at the corner of his shirt collar.

That was the last time he saw her.

Chapter 4

Connor remembered seeing the flower shop when he drove into town. As a kid, he used to save his money to buy candy at the store next to it. He had no need to buy flowers until now.

He pressed his nose against the window and peered in, imagining that he could smell the flowers. A pleasant chime sounded when Connor opened the door. The aroma of fresh flowers and the splash of bright colors greeted him. Glancing around, he didn't immediately see anyone in the shop. Every space in the small store was smartly utilized in an attractive and efficient layout.

"Hello?" a faint voice called from back of the store. "I'll be with you in a minute."

"Take your time. I'll just be looking."

A petite brunette walked out a few minutes later. "Hi. I'm Mary Ann. Can I help you?"

She was short, reaching only to the top of his shoulders. He smiled at her. "Yes, I'm Connor Norton."

"You're Connor Norton!" she said. "I was just about to call the funeral home to discuss some alternatives for your mother's arrangements. Your timing is perfect."

"I just came from there. Dale told me…there was a shortage with the flowers? I'm here to discuss other options with you."

"I'm glad you came. Please follow me, and I'll show you what we have."

She took him to the back of the store and showed him the arrangements she was working on.

"My mother's favorite color is white," Connor said. "I'd like to see what flowers you have in that color."

"Dale wasn't sure what colors to use, so I'd extra-ordered several varieties of seasonal white flowers. Here's what may work…" Mary Ann reached in the floral refrigerator and picked a selection of white flowers. She paused. "I don't have any lilies. I'm cautious about using them ever since a customer's cat almost died from lily poisoning. It doesn't take much to be potentially fatal…small ingestions of any part of the lily plant or pollen, even drinking the water from the vase."

"I didn't know lilies are so deadly. I've heard certain plants and foods are toxic to cats."

She made a new arrangement and tied it together with blue and white lace ribbons. "What do you think?"

Connor studied the arrangement. He nodded. "I think she would be very pleased."

"That's wonderful." Mary Ann's face lit up. She was eager to get back to work. "I'll add these flowers to the other arrangement, the wreath, and the table centerpiece." She looked up at him. "Would you like to come back later to look at them?"

Connor pulled out his cell phone to check the time. "I've got a few more stops to make. But I can come back later…maybe when you close?"

"That's fine. We close at five but I'm usually still here in the back till six or seven. I'll keep an eye out for you," Mary Ann said. "I'll put the CLOSED sign on the door, but I won't lock it. You can come in. I'll listen for the bell."

"Great. I'll stop by later."

Chapter 5

Connor walked out and closed the door, then headed for Mr. Monroe's office. Rocky Flats was a one-lawyer town, and Mr. Monroe did legal business for everybody. His office was prominently located in the middle of town, right next to the bank. Connor always thought Mr. Monroe situated his office there so he wouldn't have far to walk each time he deposited the money he collected from his clients in town.

He opened the door. A woman in her fifties sat behind the desk, dressed in a severe business suit. Black-rimmed glasses perched on her nose. A slight lifting of her right eyebrow was the only sign of welcome. "Yes?"

"Hi, I'm Connor Norton. I have an appointment to see Mr. Monroe."

"Oh yes, Mr. Monroe is expecting you," she said as she reached for her desk phone. "I'll tell him you're here."

"Thank you."

A minute later the door opened and Mr. Monroe himself came out. The lawyer had known the Norton family for many years and done business with Connor's father. He shook Connor's hand with enthusiasm. "Good to see you. Please come in."

He ushered Connor into his office, nodding to his secretary.

"I've been expecting you," he said.

"Hello, Mr. Monroe. I just got back in town."

"I'm very sorry to hear about your mom. My deepest condolences."

"Thank you."

"I know this has come all of a sudden. We have some business to attend to, papers to sign," said Mr. Monroe as he pulled a folder of documents from a drawer in his desk.

"You have my full attention," said Connor, sitting straight up in the brown leather chair. He felt the unforgiving stiffness of the chair and squirmed, wishing he could sink into a soft, cushioned seat before getting to business. The discomfort of the chair was nothing compared to what he was feeling inside. He wasn't ready to sign off on any big decisions now, even if Mr. Monroe insisted.

An hour later, Connor was back out and walking in the street. He turned toward the church. It was always open—a sanctuary welcoming all.

"Pastor Maller?" he called as he went into the church.

"Oh, Connor," said the pastor warmly. "How are you?"

"I'm fine," said Connor. "I'm sorry to trouble you, but I wonder if you'd say a prayer with me...for my mother."

"Of course. Please come in."

"I just left the funeral home and the flower shop. Is there anything else we need to discuss before the service?"

"Well...there is the matter of the music. Does your mother have a favorite song?"

"Oh, that's easy. 'Climb Ev'ry Mountain' was my mother's favorite."

"I happen to have that music," the pastor said with a twinkle in his eyes. "I can ask my daughter to sing this song if you'd like."

"Oh, that'll be wonderful. Please ask her."

"I'm sure she'll do it. She's sang this with your mom and knows the song well."

"My mother would absolutely love that!" Connor breathed a sigh of relief. He had not thought of the music for the funeral service and was glad the pastor had brought it up. "Could we pray together for my mother now? I'd like that."

The pastor nodded as he started the prayer.

Chapter 6

Walking back outside into the brightness of the day, Connor welcomed the afternoon sun. He raised his head, wanting the rays to penetrate deep down, awakening the parts of him dwelling in the darkness. The day so far had been somber and filled with sorrow. He needed to grieve, and he knew there would be days and days ahead when he would mourn his mother. For now, he closed his eyes and turned his face toward the sun, basking in the sunshine. He thought he felt the gentle touch of God for a moment.

Connor checked the time on his cell phone. It was 4:30. He had another stop to make at the hardware store.

"Hey, Ron," Connor called to the guy loading bags of mulch into the back of a customer's pickup. He had known Ron since Rocky Flats Elementary School.

Ron turned and, recognizing Connor, shouted, "Hey man, you're back!"

Connor reached his friend quickly with long strides and patted him on the back. "Glad to see you out here working so hard."

"Shucks, man, you should have seen the last load," he said with a chuckle. "You just got in?"

"Yep. I'll be staying at the house to get things in order."

"So how long are you planning on staying?"

"About three weeks. If I get done earlier, I may go back earlier."

"Stay for a bit if you can. We haven't seen much of you," Ron said with a grin, adding, "Even if you get done earlier."

"We'll see about that. I've got a lot of work to do back at the office."

"See you around, then," said Ron. Then he turned serious. "You know we are closing the store tomorrow...out of respect for your mother."

"Thanks, man. This means a lot...you can't imagine how much it means to me."

"Your parents were kind to me. Your dad sold me the business after I'd worked for him for over ten years."

"Yes, I know."

"I thought I could do it all, but I didn't know how much was involved in a business." He shook his head. "Don't get me wrong. I love the work, but it's a little more than I can handle."

"So what are you thinking of doing?"

"Well, I've been thinking about getting a partner, and then expanding your father's old hardware business."

"Expanding?"

"Yup. Adding an outdoor section with lawn mowers, furniture, and chain saws; a garden center with plants and more; maybe some guns and ammo. I'm also thinking about expanding the kitchen wares and adding more appliances."

"Sounds interesting. My mom would have liked the kitchen gadgets and appliances. But guns and ammo? I really don't see the need in this peaceful town."

Ron cleared his throat. "We can talk about it. I know you just got in town, but let me put it out to you now. I want to make this offer to you first, partners 50/50. It feels like it's the right thing to do."

"I appreciate this. I'd like to think it over. When do you need my answer?"

"I'll need to know by the end of the year, so don't take too long."

Connor nodded. "Thanks."

He dashed across the street to the flower shop. It felt good to be home. He didn't have to drive around town looking for everyone. People moved in a slower pace here than in the city, or so it seemed. But maybe it was just that people were more relaxed, and things felt more natural. The stress of city life seemed like a lifetime removed. Connor was determined not to think of work and just be here.

Chapter 7

"Hey, I'm back!" shouted Connor as he opened the door to the little flower shop and the bell dinged. Connor made a mental note to ask Mary Ann what the bell was made of, what metal made such an enchanting sound.

Mary Ann came from the back of the store, gesturing for him to follow her. "Here, I'd like to show you my new arrangements. Come on back."

Connor walked back, not knowing what to expect. When he got there, his eyes opened wide. "What…you did all this?"

Mary Ann had made good use of her time and her skills. The arrangements were beautiful and elegant. She had saved special blue ribbons and exquisite white lace for a time like this. *This is fit for a queen!* thought Connor.

"Well, do you like it?"

"Like it? I LOVE it!"

"I had a little creative inspiration and added tiny blue flowers in the background, and it was absolutely the right touch to accentuate the table arrangement."

"This is so lovely. Thank you!" gushed Connor as he admired her handiwork. "My mother…this is a lovely tribute…more than I expected."

"I'm glad," said Mary Ann, blushing a bit.

"Well, how can I thank you enough?" said Connor.

"You already have," said Mary Ann. "I'll have these delivered to the funeral home in the morning."

Chapter 8

Connor walked back to his SUV. He felt hungry and decided to stop at the grocery store on his way back to the house. It hadn't changed much. He quickly grabbed a few things for breakfast and dinner, plus a can of coffee and sugar. He would come back later.

Pulling up in the driveway of his family home, he couldn't help feeling sad at the way it looked, a bit neglected. The house needed a fresh coat of paint, and the yard needed work. His dad had taken care of a lot of this when he was alive. Connor parked his car, taking out his luggage and the grocery bags.

Opening the door, Connor smelled the faint odor of musk. He put his suitcase in his old bedroom and quickly ran around, opening the windows and curtains to bring in the light and fresh air. The house was orderly and neat as always. His mom had taken great care to keep it that way.

Soon Connor was heating food for his dinner, and the coffee was brewing. Connor felt exhausted and gratefully sought out the couch. He turned on the TV, but not much was on. The usual stuff…somebody got an award, the weather, upcoming activities. Not much crime here. They did announcements of birth, weddings, and deaths. Connor saw a notice come up about his mother's funeral, along with the lovely photo of her. He looked at the picture and remembered one more thing. Glancing at the clock, he hesitated, wondering if it was too late to call. He picked up the phone.

"Hello, Mr. Williams? This is Connor Norton again." He paused. "I hope it's not too late, but I just thought of something."

"No problem. How can I help you?"

"Well…you know the picture of my mother…the one that was in the paper?"

"Yes."

He nodded. "That's the one…do you have that picture for the service tomorrow?"

"I do."

"Oh, good. What size do you have?"

"Five by seven."

"Do you think it's possible to have a larger size blown up and framed for the funeral?"

"I'll see what I can do."

"Great. Oh, by the way I was at the flower shop. They will be delivering the arrangements tomorrow morning. They are very lovely," Connor added.

"Excellent. Will that be all?"

"Yes…that's all…see you tomorrow." He finished the call.

At some point after Connor ate his dinner, he dozed off on the couch. He was so tired that he didn't even make it to his room.

Chapter 9

The grating noise of the garbage truck rudely awoke him the next morning. Connor jolted, realizing that he had forgotten to put out the garbage. It was pointless to run out now, so he lay back for a moment, listening to the birds chirping. It looked like another beautiful and bright day. Sunny. No sign of rain.

Connor jumped into the shower, cleaned up, and dressed in a t-shirt and jeans. Before the afternoon service, he planned to come back to freshen up and put on his new suit—his best suit. He fixed a plate of scrambled eggs and toast. It was a light breakfast but enough for him to get started. He brewed a fresh pot of coffee, planning to drink it black. He took the paper and his cup of coffee outside to sit on the porch. Glancing through the paper, he quickly got caught up with the goings-on in the town. It was a small paper, but full of local news, events, and activities. There was a section for national and international news also, as well as comics, ads, and a crossword puzzle.

Connor smiled, recalling how many times he watched his dad grab the crossword puzzle page first. His mom would try to get his dad's attention whenever he took too long doing the puzzle. She had gotten irritated more than once at how *slow* he was. She didn't quite get it…that it was relaxing for him, that he took his time thinking about the words. Honestly, it was possible that his dad even took a little longer than necessary to do the crossword puzzle on occasion, especially if she was bugging him. Little things like not putting the toilet lid down or leaving dirty socks around bothered a lot of married folks, but with his mom and dad, he recalled them mostly arguing about the crossword puzzles.

His mom, if truth be told, felt left out whenever his dad did his crosswords. Truly, she felt he had closed a door on her. When he was doing a crossword, she'd lean over his shoulder, peer at what he'd put down on the puzzle, and sometimes she'd shout out a word or two before he could think it. But he didn't like that either. He didn't want her doing that, and he certainly didn't want her to shout out a word before he could put it down. No, no, no! That he didn't like. Connor could see this scenario playing out now…and smiled. He had watched this so many times; it was always the same thing over and over. As many times as he had seen them, they always acted as if they've never had the conversation before. It was amusing to him, but they were serious about it, utterly serious. This was a habit, a routine they did week after week, for years, as long as he could remember.

Chapter 10

It was almost lunchtime. Connor wasn't feeling hungry. Really, he was too nervous to eat. He got out his new suit and dressed slowly before driving to the funeral home. The door to the funeral home was open already. Inside, a table was laid out with brochures about his mom's service, with the eye-catching flower arrangement in the middle and the sign-in book next to it.

Entering the sanctuary, he went straight to see his mother. She was wearing the new dress and the pearls, looking beautiful at rest. A spectacular large flower arrangement was placed next to her. The enlarged eight by ten framed picture, his favorite photo of his mom, was propped on a stand, framed by the gorgeous wreath of white flowers. Everything was perfect.

Connor greeted the pastor, then sat down and waited for the service to start. People came in quietly and filled the room. Somewhere he heard the soft sounds of notes played on a flute! It was calming and echoed in the room as it floated on air. He was lost in the music, surrounded by the beauty and fragrance of the flowers. As he gazed at her picture, the happy memories flooded back. He saw his mother dancing in the field, arms out and twirling, happy and laughing. He smiled. It was as if she was singing and dancing in the meadow and in the hills. Then he heard the most pleasing sound...a voice that started low and then soared higher and higher singing, "The hills are alive with the sound of music..."

He looked around and saw the girl singing—well, she sounded like a girl, but she was a woman singing. The passion and beauty of her voice captivated him. Her face lit up like an angel singing to his mother. He imagined that his mom could hear this music and was singing along with the song she knew so well and had sung to him so many times before. He was really touched. He composed himself and fell into a trance for the rest of the song, forgetting everything else except for this special tribute to his mother.

This was the moment when he realized the beauty of it all. At that moment, he put aside the sorrow. For he was here, among all these people, in this sacred place, surrounded by beauty, music, and love...there would be no sorrow. No sorrow would be sent to her along the way where she must go now. They would send music, happiness, and love. For where she was going, there would never be any pain or sadness; there would be only eternal joy. And there, he firmly believed, she would forever rest in peace. The thought of his mother in eternal peace calmed and comforted him. She would be there waiting for him when it was his time, and she would join her ancestors. That he also believed. So he was really happy at the moment, as he should be, in this, her moment. This was the celebration of her life! A person only got to do this once. This was her moment. The world was a better place for her having lived in it. And she left her mark behind, forever, in this world.

No matter if you were a good person or a bad person, Connor truly believed that when a person leaves this world, they would have a place to go to that would either give them peace or would put them in torment for eternity because of what they did in their lifetime. Or maybe, just maybe, there was a third place, another place between the two, where they would get another chance if they really wanted to be a better person—there would be another way to get a second chance…not in this life, but in the next life, in the middle place…in-between the other two places. Maybe.

But Connor had to believe in something, in the balance of the world or how it all worked. Maybe the good, bad, beautiful, and ugly all had to be balanced. The world wasn't all good or all bad, and it wasn't all beautiful or all ugly. Maybe in the next place there would still be all of this; maybe there would be a chance to have another life that turned the bad into the good or the ugly into the beautiful. Because if everything was the same, then all would be the same. There would be no souls to save if all souls were good. There would be no ugliness if all were beautiful. Would we get tired of it if everyone and everything was good and beautiful? Would we appreciate what each person had if we didn't have anything else? Would anyone know what it was like to be bad or ugly? Would we feel the angst of those who yearned to be, even for one day, good and beautiful? Who would yearn to be bad and ugly? Maybe there would be people who would yearn for that? That and everything in between. Connor's thoughts rambled on and on.

Was there an afterlife? Could he know for sure that she'd never feel the cold? Or the pain? Would he meet her again one day when he was also gone from this world? He wouldn't know the answers until he took the journey, whatever path he would be on. Who knew the path and where it would take him? He would have to see.

The music had stopped. The pastor was speaking, Connor quickly realized. At first he didn't catch the words, but he felt them. The way the pastor was talking, the feeling he was expressing, was so eloquent, so beautiful. Connor didn't have to listen to the words to catch the meaning. It was obvious that it was a tribute to someone dear. The dearly departed mother that Connor so loved. She would have liked it if she could have heard. She would have enjoyed hearing his stories and what he shared.

Connor had chosen not to speak at her service. He wanted to pay his respects quietly and privately. He couldn't imagine getting up in front of all these people, what he would say. He felt a twinge of guilt. He had left twenty years ago and only came back infrequently, staying a few days at a time. Most visits were during the holidays, the obligatory times. A few times he came home for important events like birthdays, anniversaries, or whenever he could make it home. It wasn't like he even knew everybody anymore. He felt like a stranger. Then again, he had changed over the years, and folks who remembered Connor as a child no longer recognized him. His guilt was mixed with regret, with remorse that he hadn't come back as often or stayed as long as he should have. He had become more distant from his dad. Initially, he had pulled back to work out some of his issues. Over the years, the resentment kept him at bay, and he barely spoke to his dad when he came home. His dad was a man of few words anyway, but even so it was noticeable that they hardly talked. There was no meanness between them, just a thin veil of ice that could not be warmed over. His mother pleaded with him, but Connor was stubborn. There were times he looked in his mother's eyes and saw her love. He knew she wanted to see more of him, that she missed him; she didn't even have to say it. He knew that no matter what, no matter how far away he was, she loved him. He loved her too, but he didn't really say it as he should have. It was something he would have to live with. There was nothing he could do about it now.

Connor went through the rest of the service, his memories wandering in and out, not quite sure what he had heard but lost in his thoughts, thinking things that he wanted to say to his mother if she were here. He heard quiet sniffles. Here and there a muffled sob could be heard. Others had tears on their faces and dabbed with tissues or handkerchiefs. He watched as more people expressed their grief. He came out of his grief to join the rest of the congregation in their collective grief, all the while rejoicing her life.

The service was coming to an end and he could hear the music once again. The flute played; this time it was joined by a violin, and together the notes became a melodious symphony of joyous sounds. The music uplifted and calmed, it flowed and soothed, until his heart was salved, this passage was taken, this tribute done, and her life was honored.

He stood as the service ended. People came up to talk to him, and he went through the motions, greeting each and hearing their words of comfort. The words blended together. Sounding alike and yet distinct. He was polite and thanked everyone for coming. He didn't attempt to smile except for the few times when he returned a smile. Connor stood by her as people came to pay their last respects. It was quiet, orderly, and people even whispered so as not to disturb her rest.

He had a choice of burial or cremation. It wasn't something they had talked about, but he remembered one conversation where he had overheard his mother talking at another funeral, telling someone she was glad there would be a burial. There was something so physically final about totally letting go, scattering ashes to the wind, to the earth, or to the sea. Yes, it was something he had thought about. But a part of him also didn't want to do that. Burial was a time-honored way to go.

He knew she would be buried here, next to his father, in her best new dress and the pearls. He would have a place to come visit her. He could touch the ground, touch her headstone, and know that she was safe in her resting place. He had already purchased a plot next to his mom to prepare for his own journey. He knew that each day he had in the world was one less day that he would have to live, and that each day he lived took him closer to where he was going. He didn't know when or how or where it would happen. But he knew it was inevitable. As life was inevitable, so surely was death. He would be her child forever. She would be his mother forever. Nothing would ever change that. Ever.

Chapter 11

Connor slept in the next morning. He didn't have appointments or activities scheduled. He was going to let the day unfold, see how it went, and not plan anything. He still had three weeks minus two days at home.

One of the things Connor knew he had to do was to go over their belongings. His parents didn't have a lot of things, or it didn't seem like it. But looking over the house, he realized they had more than he had thought. There were several filing cabinets and boxes of stuff in the attic as well.

He stretched his legs and got out of bed. He took his time making breakfast. While the coffee was brewing, he went out on the porch and got the paper. He absentmindedly checked the classified section. He did this in the city, checking out jobs whenever he could, just to see what was out there and see what skills were in demand. He was really on top of his game, some people would say.

But there wasn't a large classified section in this paper, just a few postings. He hadn't expected to see a lot. A few handyman ads, some yard work, odds and ends. There was an ad for a part-time assistant to help with bookkeeping and paperwork. It didn't give the name of the business, just a number to call. He looked at the next section and saw some items for sale. That seemed like a good idea for the stuff he would have to sell. As a matter of fact, he hadn't even thought about what he would do about the house either. Yes, the house.

He made a mental list of the things he had to do; the list was getting longer and longer. The three weeks were suddenly shrinking—so much to do and so little time! *No, don't worry*, he thought. This was his forte! Doing things in so little time. He could do this. There might be other things he hadn't thought of. He would have to factor that in as well. The thought of rest and relaxation vanished into thin air. *Oh, this is not happening!* He should have asked for four weeks off at the onset instead of three. He quickly rolled up his shirt sleeves. He was not wasting any more time.

First, Connor decided to take inventory and see what could be discarded, sold, or kept. If things were old, he would throw them away. As for some of the other things, better yet, he'd rather donate than sell them; that would also save a lot of time. Besides, it would be more personally satisfying than making money from his parents' belongings. Donating to someone who could use the things, who needed the things, was the way to go. Connor grabbed a sheet of paper and jotted down his plan. He got another sheet and started making a list of everything he had to do, putting a big star next to the more important items. He reviewed the list and revised it until he was satisfied.

List in hand, he walked around the house, taking another quick inventory before getting started. The plan should be workable, if he kept to the schedule. He was determined to make use of all his time here and get everything done. He hoped to make the right decisions and honor his parents while he was at it.

Connor took another sheet of paper and made a shopping list of needed items. He had to get boxes, tape, and trash bags for the things he was going to donate, keep, or throw out. He also added a note to check everything in the attic. The walk up stairs to the attic made it easier to bring things down. There were a few pieces of furniture up there, but he wasn't worried about that. He would get those later; they would probably be the last things he'd handle from the attic. A fair number of boxes were stored up there. Some were labeled and some were not. He had no idea what was up there; he would have to find out by opening the boxes one by one. The thought of doing that didn't strike his fancy, but he was determined to plow through as best as he could. He wanted to honor his parents and pay his respects. The thought of hiring some stranger to haul all their possessions away, without even looking at anything, seemed brutally cold and disrespectful.

Chapter 12

Absorbed in thought, Connor didn't hear the knock at the door the first time. It sounded again. He rushed to the door.

"Oh, hi Connor…sorry to disturb you. I'm your mother's next door neighbor," said a grey-haired woman. Her hair was pulled up in a bun and a cat was nestled in her arms.

"Oh, hi Mrs. Rainer. Please…do come in."

"I'm just dropping by," she said almost apologetically. "When this happened, I took little Tom in. I thought I'd keep him for a few days…you know… until things settled." She shifted her foot then reached out to hand Tom over to Connor. "Here…"

It took Connor a minute to figure out what she meant. He had quite forgotten about Tom. Up until now, he hadn't even thought about Tom or where he was or what happened to him.

"Hmm…Mrs. Rainer," he stumbled. "I'm quite thankful that you kept Tom for a few days." He reached out to take the cat. Tom jumped out of her arms and onto the floor, acting as if he owned the place before leaping on the couch and curling up. *Well…this is his home!* Connor reminded himself with a smile. Now that Tom was here, Connor could sure use the company. He knew how much his mom had loved Tom and pampered him. There were only so many times he could listen to her rave about how special the cat was. But now he was happy to see him. "Thank you, Mrs. Rainer."

"I'm right next door. If you have any questions, just come by." She took a step closer and whispered, "I miss her too…"

"I know."

Mrs. Rainer turned around and, as she walked out, picked up a bag of cat food she had placed next to the door. "Here, you'll need this. This is Tom's favorite food."

Connor grabbed the bag. "Thanks, ma'am."

"Oh, Connor…one more thing…"

"Yes, ma'am?"

"Just call me Dorothy…better yet, Dottie for short."

"You bet…ahem…Dottie."

She nodded in approval and left.

Chapter 13

Connor took the cat food into the kitchen. As he passed Tom, he rattled the bag. "Hey, fella, are ya hungry?"

Tom didn't pay him any mind, not even to perk up his ears at the sound of the food. Obviously he had just been fed. Otherwise, he would have come running. Connor knew this much about Tom. The thought of Tom keeping him company for the next three weeks cheered him up. He had grown up with cats because of his mother's love for them.

At one point his dad had insisted on his right to have a dog, so, briefly amid all the cats there was a single dog—a yellow fur-ball that was lovable and so cute as a puppy. Well, that didn't last long, as the puppy quickly grew up to be a good size, a medium-sized dog in the fifty-pound range. Connor loved that dog. He played with him, and they ran in the meadow together. In a small town, folks let their dogs run in the fields. Connor couldn't recall ever seeing dogs tied up in the country like he saw in the city. The dog—*his dog,* was how he thought of him—was named Olive. He was the sweetest dog and a wonderful companion. Perfect for a little boy.

Olive loved to chase, not just Connor but almost any moving thing. One day, when Connor came home from school, he could not find Olive. He looked everywhere but didn't see him. Olive would usually come running to greet him. Connor wanted to tell Olive when he left that morning that he wished he could take him to school. He wanted to explain that the school wouldn't allow that, so Olive had to stay behind. Olive looked so sad sometimes when Connor left. Connor couldn't wait to come home to see Olive. So that day, when Olive didn't come to meet him, Connor knew something was very wrong.

No one said anything to him for a while, until Connor couldn't take it anymore. Then his dad put him gently on his lap and said, "I'm sorry. So very sorry."

Connor knew, and his heart sank. He started crying; he was scared; he didn't want to hear; he didn't want anything to have happened to Olive.

"I want to tell you that it was quick," his dad said. He was a man of few words, but that day he said more than Connor had ever heard him say. "Olive had run outside to go across the street to play with a child. A pickup truck whipped around the corner and came charging up the street, going faster than he had a *goddamn* right to." Connor's dad paused to control his anger. Then he whispered, "Olive never saw it coming."

Connor cried for his dog, demanding over and over again, "I want Olive. I want my Olive!" He thought if he asked for him so many times, the universe would give him what he wanted. He cried, "I want Olive!" until his voice turned hoarse.

From that day on, Connor never asked for another dog.

They buried Olive and said a prayer. His parents never spoke of Olive again. And that was it.

Chapter 14

Connor sat down next to Tom on the couch. "How are you, old man? You must be, what, about four years old now?" he said as he playfully stroked Tom's back. "I know, you're not exactly an old man, but I'm calling you an old man just to bug ya!"

Tom turned over on his back and offered his soft underbelly. Connor tickled and stroked the cat's belly just the way he liked. In no time at all, he had Tom *purrrring*. If Tom could smile, he would have a huge smile plastered on his face. For extra, Connor threw in the ears…stroking behind each ear. He was giving Tom the royal treatment. This was what he had to offer: a really fine homecoming. He couldn't resist picking Tom up and holding him close to his chest, feeling the warmth of his little body and the soft hairs touching his cheek and tickling his nose. "Oh Tom, I'm so glad you're home," he cried out softly before giving Tom a quick rub on the cheeks for good measure.

Tom returned the favor and put his paws out, first stretching and then touching Connor's nose. Connor wiggled his nose and shook Tom's paws playfully, knowing that Tom would never hurt him. He loved Tom. It was so good to have Tom home. He made a mental note to be sure to thank Mrs. Rainer—Dottie—again as he gently put Tom back on the couch, where he curled up and settled in a nook. Yes, Tom was home and he was going to stay.

Tom was mostly an indoor cat, but he had his moments when he wanted out to chase butterflies or go after a mouse. Connor remembered the time he came home and saw a dead mouse on the doormat outside the house. He almost had a fright. But it turned out that it was Tom who had carried the dead mouse in his mouth and laid it on the front door mat for all to see. That was Tom's gift. It was what he had to offer and what he gave them.

Connor's mom had taken care of it. She even made a big fuss over Tom, telling him how wonderful he was to give them this gift. She thanked Tom by giving him special treats. She went overboard with it, Connor thought at the time. But he kept his thoughts to himself. Later, he saw his mom wrap the dead mouse in newspaper and take it out to the trash can. So much for Tom's gift.

Tom was truly a beautiful cat. He was a tabby, all stripes and orange with huge green eyes and long whiskers. Tom had a thing that he liked to do, putting his paws on door knobs to open doors. Connor had never seen any other cat do this, and he was convinced of Tom's superior intellect. Other cats never made the connection between the knobs and opening doors.

Watching Tom lick his paws one by one amused Connor. He liked that cats were self-cleaning and fastidious. But for the life of him, he couldn't figure out why they would have anything to do with dirty little rats or mice. Maybe cats didn't get the message that those critters…no, scratch that…those *rodents* carried disease and germs. Tom would have to be pretty quick to catch them, with his wits and legs primed for the chase. Connor had never seen Tom in action, but he knew that he was good…so very good. Fifteen times, if you're counting.

Chapter 15

Connor added a few things to his shopping list, including a special welcome-home treat for Tom. He added a few toys as well. There was no reason why he shouldn't pamper him a bit; after all, he was special. "Hey Tom, I'm going shopping...you hold the fort now." It was silly, but he felt good saying it. Talking to Tom like he was family...well, they were a family, living together. He loved it.

On the way to the store, Connor felt really good. He decided that the rest of the day was going to be his and Tom's alone. They would enjoy each other's company, catch up on old times, and just relax. That sounded terrific, and he was looking forward to it. Tomorrow would come soon enough, with all the work, the worries, and the stress of tackling his to-do list. Money was no problem, as he had plenty. He knew his parents' house was paid off, so he didn't have to think about a mortgage. As for Tom, that was a no-brainer. He would take Tom wherever he went. He had already decided he would take Tom with him when he went back to the city. For Tom was all the family Connor had now. He would miss Tom if he left without him. As for his condo, having cats was no problem. There were several cats in the complex already. Tom would even have other cats to play with, although he wasn't sure Tom would like that. He might like to have the place to himself. He had grown up in the house by himself.

So Tom was like an only child, except he was an only cat. Connor would keep Tom and not add other cats to the household. One was enough for now. Tom would probably be all he could handle anyway. He'd just have to get used to living indoors in the smaller quarters of the condo. That would be an adjustment for Tom; he'd have to accommodate to a bit of down-sizing when he went to Connor's home. Connor would make sure there was a perch on the window for Tom to look out and watch his comings and goings. He'd make sure the window was up a crack so Tom could feel the breeze come in through the window screen. The upstairs bedroom window would work for that. Connor was busy making plans for Tom to stay with him. He was going to keep him safe and take care of him, for as long as he lived. That was a promise.

Chapter 16

Saturday morning, Connor went shopping. He was so absorbed in his thoughts and focused on finding the cat food aisle that he bumped into another cart. "Oh, I'm so sorry!" said a startled Connor as he looked up from the cart. Recognizing Mary Ann, he asked, "Are you okay?"

She laughed. "I'm fine. You look like you're in a hurry," she said. "Need some help?"

"I'm…uh…I'm just picking up some cat food and treats for my cat."

"You have a cat…you just got here?"

"It's my mother's cat. His name is Tom."

"That's a cute name. I have a cat too. Her name is Isabella."

"Oh, maybe Isabella would like to meet Tom sometime?"

"Ha," she said. "That could be arranged." She looked at him. "You can call me."

"Yeah, let's do that. I gotta run…Tom is waiting for me at home."

Chapter 17

When Connor got home, Tom was exactly where he had left him. As Connor put away his groceries, he wistfully thought that was what he wanted to do: sleep the day away. But he knew better. With a sigh, he started to tackle the stuff in the first room. He had bought tags to label furniture to be donated and boxes to be thrown out or kept. After a while, he had a system. Soon Connor was absorbed in the process, throwing stuff in different piles: donate, discard, or keep. This would be his first sweep. After he got the easy stuff out of the way, he'd take time to go through the to-keep pile. Connor made steady progress and worked at a fast clip. By suppertime, he had already gone through one room. Satisfied, he stopped to eat and rest.

Hearing the shaking of the cat food bag, Tom flew into the kitchen and *meowed*. He zoomed right to the cat dish and got a few treats, along with the dinner Connor had put out. The water bowl was clean and full, but Tom paid no attention to it. Connor started humming and really felt good about this day. Monday he would call the donation place to arrange for the first pick-up; he would have to do that a few times to get the furniture and other stuff moved out. That would free up more space for him to work. He had already stacked up several boxes of paper and files in the to-save pile. It would take a while to go through them. It wasn't his favorite thing to do. He was saving that for last. He was relieved to have these few days to himself. He really needed this break, and there was no one else that could, and should, be doing this.

His mother...he hadn't thought of her while he was working, which took his mind off his grief. He was thankful for this distraction, for this work, and plunged into it. He had promised his mother that he wouldn't just toss out everything. He knew that would upset her. One of the neighbors, an old man who lived alone, had died. He didn't have any close relatives. Afterward, they came into his house and took everything out. They discarded most of the stuff, and there wasn't much of anything left. Then they bulldozed the house until not a scrap of wood or a sliver of windowpane was left. Nothing...just a flattened lot, a vacant and empty space where his house had once stood. There was no service or funeral. Later there was an impromptu memorial held on his lawn. People brought food and drinks, and a grill was started for burgers and hot dogs. Although many people said kind words...Connor knew that some of them had said mean words when the old man was alive. But, in the end, they honored him by coming to his memorial.

Connor wondered what a person would be like and be doing in the next world. Perhaps they would be looking down on us and seeing everything. Maybe where they went, everyone would be the same. Nobody would be rich or poor. They wouldn't use money; there would be no need. Everyone would arrive empty-handed. So what they would use or not use was a mystery. Or maybe everyone would have no needs or wants. They would just be.

Connor wondered if they existed as some kind of ghost or apparition. Or what if there was no form, just energy? Or perhaps the entity was just a spirit that had no form, that just was…and didn't take on any physical presence? Would they be spirits or something else? Connor believed something had to be there to tell the universe you had existed. People couldn't just exist in this world and that was it. If you had no place to go after this, then you had to do everything you wanted to do here, in this world.

Connor shook his head; he didn't know the answers, and he didn't know anyone else who would know the answers. The only ones who absolutely knew were those who had left this world. They would be able to tell whether this world was it, if their life, their existence, was wholly within this world. If they had another existence or another world after this, what would that be?

Connor was not some famous academic who had spent decades studying this or pouring over ancient books and researching ancient lands. He was just Connor, an ordinary man with ordinary questions about life and death. He remembered his mother saying, "Live each day well." He liked that. But he couldn't live each day to the fullest in that sense of the word when he spent his days…well, his long days and evenings with his work. That wouldn't be called living each day well, not by any stretch of the imagination.

Connor was alone in this world. He let that thought sink in. He had not wanted to face this before. He always had a home to come to. He had never wanted to think about the inevitable, that some day they wouldn't be here, and there would be no one to come home to. Or, that there would be no home at all. An empty house was not a home. It was not even close. Grappling with his thoughts, he focused on what he had to do now. Grief was pushed aside momentarily as he threw himself back into work.

Chapter 18

The next few days passed quickly. Connor moved methodically from one room to the next. The donation truck came by several times to pick up furniture, clothes, books, and other items. The garbage can was loaded and surrounded by piles of trash bags, which all got picked up. Connor made quick work going through the big stuff while putting all the to-save piles together in one room. He would have to go through them and decide if anything was worth keeping.

His mom kept a lot of his stuff: his first tooth, his first school paper, his first A on an exam, his drawings, and all his birthday and Happy Mother's Day cards. It was so nice to have it all there. She didn't place them in a scrapbook, but she had kept everything together. He would take that with him. Then there was other stuff: financial papers, mortgage, insurance, taxes, and other documents. He would make another appointment with the attorney to take care of some of this. The house was paid for. He was proud of his parents. They weren't frivolous folks. There was little discretionary money for fun or fancy items, furniture, or clothes. But he never felt poor growing up. He had a roof over his head, clothes, shoes, and enough to eat. His mom made delicious home-cooked meals and packed his lunch at the same time. His lunch wasn't leftovers technically because his lunch wasn't left over from what was cooked at dinner. She packed his lunch first, and then they had dinner. She always made enough and made sure there was extra food for his lunch. She didn't believe in sandwiches. She thought they were boring. How many variations of a sandwich could you make when you knew each time it would be two slices of bread with lunchmeat and cheese in the middle?

She tried to make healthy food for him. She would go to the farmer's market or make delicious meals out of vegetables from their garden. He made it a point to always eat the lunch his mother made for him.

What Connor looked for, more than any other item in his lunchbox, was her homemade doughnuts. He loved her yummy glazed doughnuts and the ones drizzled with chocolate icing. At certain times in the fall, he'd get pumpkin doughnuts. But the doughnuts decorated with her colorful homemade, animal-shaped gummies were super special. Whenever his mom made these delectable treats, he became quite popular at lunchtime and never lacked for kids who wanted to make a trade with their lunches. When they found out that didn't work, they would bring in other items for trade, like a toy or something he didn't have.

The more well-to-do kids even offered money to him. He never took money.

Since he was ahead of schedule, Connor allowed himself a treat, take the rest of the day off. He needed this time to relax, to regroup. Leaving his car in the driveway, he decided to take a walk. The day was beautiful, the clouds were white and fluffy, and there was a slight breeze. He wanted to get out of the house and stretch his legs. Where else could you leave your house and walk with the birds singing overhead, the trees and leaves gently swaying, past the meadows and fields and wildflowers and past the tidy houses with the picket fences? Connor enjoyed every minute of it, taking in the beauty around him, and smelling the fresh air.

Ahhhh…this was heaven on earth.

Chapter 19

As he walked for the first time in years, he realized twenty years had gone by in a flash. Where had all the time gone? Where was he in those twenty years? With a slight pang of remorse, he calculated how many walks he could have taken: 365 days a year times 20 years was 7,300 days. That was a lot of walks.

"Hey, Connor!"

Connor looked around and saw the neighbor Mrs. Rainer outside working. "Hi, Mrs. Rainer…er, Dottie."

"Come here and talk to me a bit," she said as she waved him over.

"Yeah."

"I've been meaning to clip these bushes and trim them a bit. They grow pretty fast," she said. She moved to one side, eyeing her work. "Tell me, from where you stand, do the bushes look straight?"

Connor studied her work, moving his eyes in an imaginary line across the tops of the bushes. "Let's see...I think a bit of trim at the top there," he said as he pointed. "That would do it."

She clipped them and stepped back to look. "There, that does look better."

Connor nodded.

"Thanks, Connor."

"No problem. Hey, I want to thank you again for taking care of Tom. I am enjoying spending time with him," said Connor.

"Well, I'm glad to hear that. Tom appeared at your mother's doorstep one day. She took him in." She paused to reflect. "You should have seen him that first day...he was scraggly and thin, shivering from the rain. Real sorry looking."

"I would never know from looking at him now. He's the picture of health and getting a little pudgy, I think," said Connor, laughing.

"Yes, Tom has put on a few pounds and then some, but he's still fit and in his prime."

"Cat years are seven to every human year, right?"

"That's what they say."

"So that makes him...four times seven is twenty-eight years old," Connor calculated. "Why, he's younger than I am...in cat years, I mean."

"That's right."

Pleased with this, Connor grinned from ear to ear. "That makes my day!"

"Glad to hear that…have a good day, Connor."

"You too, Dottie," Connor said as he resumed his walk; this time there was a little lilt to his steps.

Chapter 20

Connor had just gotten home when the phone rang. "Hello?"

"Hi, this is Pastor Maller. How are you doing?"

"I'm good. I've been keeping busy. How are you?"

"I'm fine. Well, I thought you may want to pick up your mother's picture. I still have it."

"Yes, of course. I'd like that. Are you going to be there?"

"I will be for a little while, then I have a home visitation. But I'll leave the picture in my office. The door to the church is open. My daughter will be here if you need help."

"Okay. I'll be by to pick it up. Thanks."

Connor grabbed a bite to eat for lunch, before picking up his car keys and heading out. It was a short drive to the church. He went straight to the pastor's office. The door was open, and he poked his head in.

The pastor wasn't there but a woman was sitting in his chair typing on his computer. He knocked. "Hello?"

"Oh, hello." She looked up with a smile. "You must be Connor. My dad said you'd be coming by to pick up your mother's picture."

"Yes, I'm Connor," he said, extending his hand to shake hers.

"I'm Eva."

"I recognize you from the service, your beautiful voice," said Connor. "I was touched. I loved the way you sang mother's favorite songs."

"I learned those songs from your mother. I used to visit her and she'd play the records of her favorite songs. We'd sing them together over and over."

"Oh, I didn't know that."

"I know those songs by heart. When I sing them, I imagine that she's right here with me, and that we're singing them together…like we used to." Her voice broke; she paused and then continued, "I miss her a lot."

"I miss her too. Going over her things, in her house, has brought back a lot of memories."

"I know."

Connor suddenly had a thought. "Listen, would you like to have her records and the phonograph? I couldn't think of a better person."

She flashed a smile. "Why Connor, I'd love to! Thank you."

"I've got another idea. Why don't you and your dad come over for supper tonight…if you are free? I haven't thanked you yet."

"I'm sure Dad would love that. I think we are both free tonight…he was just asking if I needed anything from the grocery store on his way back."

"Well come on over tonight. How does seven sound?"

"Sounds good. We'll be there."

"Great, see you then." Connor waved as he headed out to the market to get things for the dinner.

Chapter 21

One thing Connor was for sure good about: he was a good cook. All those years of watching his mother prepare dinner and his lunch came to good use. At first he had just watched, and then gradually his mom let him help. By the time he was about nine years old, he was making dinner with her, and sometimes she'd let him make dishes by himself. This had really helped him over the years. He was good at whipping things up from scratch, or creating something new from the leftovers. Even his mother said he was a good cook. Over the years, since he'd left home, he had gotten away from this. Cooking for just himself was not as much fun, and he didn't make anything elaborate. He made simple, quick meals that didn't need a lot of preparation. He cherished those times they cooked together when he came home during Thanksgiving and Christmas holidays. This brought back old memories, good memories. He slid into that role like he had never left it. Happy times definitely centered on food in this house.

Connor stopped by the farmer's market for some fresh produce. He already had a vision of what to make and picked up what he needed. He had plenty of time. It was something he looked forward to. Today he was going to do something he enjoyed with the nicest people coming over for dinner. He was going to make a home-cooked meal. On his way back, he passed by the flower shop and remembered meeting Mary Ann at the store the other day. He hesitated and then decided to run in. She was finishing up an order with another customer. She acknowledged him with a smile. "It'll just be a moment."

As soon as the customer left, he said, "Hi, I was in the neighborhood…thought I'd drop by and take you up on your offer."

"Oh, that's nice. Let's see…do you mean your offer for Isabella to meet Tom?" she said as she laughed.

"Hmm, you got that right. So…how about it? Would tonight at seven work? I'm making dinner and invited the pastor and his daughter. Would you like to come?"

"I'd love to. Really that's very nice of you to invite me. I'll bring my cat also; she can dine with Tom."

"Okay then, see you at seven."

"Would you like me to bring something or help? I'm a good cook."

"No need to bring anything…I picked up what I needed from the market. I wouldn't think of asking you to help."

"I don't mind. How about I come a little early, say around six since you wouldn't let me bring anything?"

"Well if you insist, then come at six. I wouldn't mind some help." Connor looked at his watch. "It's 3:30, so I'll see you in about two and a half hours."

He had two more stops to make to buy some wine and to invite Mrs. Rainer. He didn't know if anyone drank wine, especially the pastor and his daughter. But he wanted to have some on hand, just in case. He didn't know if Mrs. Rainer would come, but she lived alone, and he definitely wanted to include her.

Chapter 22

He got home and quickly went to work, rolling his sleeves up and washing his hands to his elbows. Mrs. Rainer had said she'd come. He did a quick count: there would be five.

"Hey Tom, you're in for a surprise tonight."

Tom was not the least bit interested. He just looked at Connor like, *Huh? What are you talking about?*

"Yes, Tom, you'll have a visitor. I know you aren't used to having other cats around, but Isabella is coming for a visit."

Tom looked bored. He was going back to sleep. Ha!

Connor quickly got started, laying out the ingredients and the cutting board. He didn't know what anyone liked, so he planned to have a variety of dishes and a salad. He got to work chopping and cutting. The time went quickly.

Knock knock knock.

He looked at the clock. It was six already! He wiped his hands and went to open the door. "Come in, Mary Ann. I see you brought—"

"Yes, I brought Isabella. I see Tom is on the couch."

Tom was quite attentive now, his ears perked up and eyes wide open. He surveyed the scene, paying special attention to the little white cat perched on Mary Ann's arms. Watching. *On full alert.* Never taking his eyes off the cat.

"Let me introduce them," she said as she walked toward Tom. Isabella chose that moment to wiggle and struggle, but Mary Ann held on. "Whoa…just wait a minute."

Tom started to move, poised to jump off the couch or make a dash to some other area. He really didn't want to move; this was his couch, his house. But he didn't want to be next to some strange cat either. He sniffed as she got closer.

The other cat had her eyes on Tom. As Isabella struggled to jump out of Mary Ann's arms, she was watching Tom to see what he would do. *The couch looks comfy*, she thought. *Wouldn't mind crashing on that.* She preferred the couch to the floor. Mary Ann brought her a little closer, and then slowly eased away to a safer distance, while both cats watched each other. She gently set her cat down on the other end of the couch. Tom relaxed a bit and curled up in his original position, settling back in his place on the sofa.

He wasn't going to have to move after all. He sighed with relief. He kept his eyes on the other cat, just in case she made a move toward him, horning in on his territory. *He wasn't going to have any of that! He was going to stay in his spot. Let her leave if she didn't like it. He was just fine where he was.*

"Well, that's settled." Mary Ann said, straightening up. She walked over to the sink and washed up. "I picked up some fruit on the way here."

Connor took the fruit and washed it as he updated her on the menu and the various stages of cooking. The broccoli casserole was in the oven. The potatoes were already peeled. He was getting ready to make the salad and spaghetti when she had arrived.

"Let me do the salad. I'll cut up the apples and add some walnuts."

Connor got out another cutting board and moved over to give her room. "I'm almost done with the potatoes. I'll start the water for the spaghetti."

Mary Ann fit right in. Connor was glad to have her help. It reminded him of the days when he worked with his mom in this kitchen. The warmth of the kitchen, the aroma of food cooking, and the clinking of pots and pans made it so much more fun. He peeked over at the couch to see how Tom and her cat were doing. All was quiet on the couch front. No fights yet. At least they seemed to be getting along for now.

Chapter 23

At seven, Mrs. Rainer came right on time. "Hello, Mrs. Rainer, do come in," Connor greeted her warmly and introduced Mary Ann and Isabella. "I'd like to offer you the couch, but right now the chair is all I have."

She glanced at Tom and Isabella on the couch. "Oh, that's quite all right. I see Tom has made himself quite at home, and he has a visitor."

The pastor and his daughter came right behind her while the door was still open. Connor welcomed them and ushered them in. "You know Mrs. Rainer?"

"Yes, of course, hello," the pastor said.

"And this is Mary Ann."

"From the flower shop?"

"Yes."

"I think we're about ready. So why don't we move to the dining room and have a seat?" Connor said.

Connor sat at the head of the table. The pastor and his daughter sat on one side of the table. Mary Ann and Mrs. Rainer sat on the other side. "The seat on the end is reserved for Tom, should he choose to join us at the table," said Connor. Everyone chuckled, and that broke the ice.

They started with the salad; it was a fresh and tasty blend of mixed greens, dried cranberries, fresh apple slices, walnuts, and blue cheese crumbles with homemade strawberry balsamic vinaigrette dressing.

There was plenty of food. Everything was delicious. Connor turned to Mary Ann next to him. "Thanks for your help today."

"I enjoyed it." She smiled.

"I want to thank each one of you for being a part of my mother's life and what you did in the beautiful funeral service," Connor said to the group. "I can't thank you enough." He paused. "I know I haven't been home much in the last twenty years, but you have been here. You have known my mother and father and been their friends. I am touched by your kindness at the service through your words, music, and flowers. Each of you is special to my mother and me...and Tom, too." He cleared his throat. "I know my mother lives within us and that her memories live in all of us. I'm not much for speeches, so that's all I have to say."

Pastor Maller spoke next. "I've known your mother the longest, and I will truly miss her."

His daughter added, "I cherished the time I spent with her, the music we shared, the songs we sang, and we even danced as we sang." She paused. "Thank you."

"Connor, I never thought your mother would leave this world before me. We had grown close, especially after your father and my husband passed. She was my neighbor and my friend. I think about her and miss her," Mrs. Rainer said softly.

Mary Ann was the last to speak. "Your mother ordered the flowers for your dad's funeral. She made all the arrangements and handled the details for his service. I hadn't been here that long when I first met her. She made me feel especially welcome, and she told all her friends about my flower shop. I'll never forget that."

Connor looked around the table. He was warmed by their presence and love, and for the first time since his mother passed, he felt at home. Lived in. "Thank you for making this a home and for being here today. You don't know how much this means to me." He wiped a tear from the corner of his eye, quickly stood up, and went in the kitchen.

"Now, here's what you've been waiting for…the decadent dessert," Connor said as he reappeared a few minutes later.

"Ahhh…" someone murmured as he brought out a five-layer chocolate cake with whipped butter cream frosting and put it on the table; it was as delectable as it looked.

"I'm putting on a pot of coffee…anyone want a cup?"

Four hands went up.

He put the cream and sugar on the table along with the mugs. The coffee brewed quickly, and Connor poured everyone a cup. "There's more if you want it."

They took their time, relaxing over dessert. The soft murmurs, the subdued clinking of silverware on the plates…it was like music to Connor's ears. He was grateful for the people and the good food. He didn't bring out the wine; he had thought better of it after he got home. As it turned out, he didn't really need it. Everything worked out fine.

He wanted this to go on and on; he didn't want to let this end. After a while, Mrs. Rainer got up. "I'm afraid it's past my bedtime now. You young folks stay and have fun."

Connor stood up. "Let me walk you home, it's past nine and I don't want you out there alone."

"Oh, all right. But you don't have to. This neighborhood is pretty safe." She headed for the door and paused to let Connor to catch up. "Bye Tom, I hope you had fun too," she said with a twinkle in her eyes as she watched Tom chasing the other cat and scurrying under the couch.

"Tom has found a new friend." Connor laughed, delighted to see Tom having fun.

Chapter 24

When Connor got back, the dishes had been washed and music was playing. Eva had brought out the records. His mom had added to her collection since he had left. Connor had not heard these songs for some time; some of the records were quite old. The music livened up the place.

Eva and Mary Ann were dancing. They looked over at Connor. "Come and join us!" Eva called.

"Oh, I'm not much of a dancer. I really am not," Connor said shyly. "If it's okay with you, I'd rather watch."

"Come on, Connor," said Eva as she danced toward him. "Just try it. You don't have to know any steps. You can just shake your bootie…arm…finger… or whatever you want to shake."

"Come join us," chimed Mary Ann as she kicked up her heels. She had taken her shoes off and was dancing barefoot.

What the heck, Connor thought as he joined them. Maybe a little music was what he needed.

After a few songs, he really got into it. Connor got lost in the music and the energy of the dance. He couldn't remember the last time he had danced. He loosened up his body and relaxed his mind and just let go. It was exhilarating, liberating, and so much fun. It made tonight even more special, and he wished—no, he *knew* that his mother would be watching them with a pleased smile. This was how she would have wanted him to live. To dance, to dream, to live!

The dancing went on for quite a while. Connor was the first to stop. He was huffing and puffing. Eva and Mary Ann laughed when he shook his head, put his hands up, and backed out. After another song or two, they also flopped on the couch, out of breath. Connor went to the refrigerator and grabbed bottles of flavored water for everyone.

Connor glanced over at the clock and saw that it was now about 10:30 P.M. Pastor Maller was dozing in his chair. Mary Ann caught his eye, yawned, and said, "It's past my bedtime."

Eva woke the pastor and met up with Mary Ann at the door. Connor hugged and thanked them. "I'm so glad you came; this was very special."

"Oh, I almost forgot. I have to get my cat," Mary Ann said as she rushed past him, back into the house.

"I'll help you find her."

Chapter 25

By this time the pastor and his daughter had waved good-bye and were out the door. The cats were still playing some game. They weren't in the living room. Connor made a quick pass through the rooms but didn't see them. He even took a look under the bed and under the dressers. Nope, they weren't there. He called out to Mary Ann as he headed toward the attic. "Maybe they're up here."

Running up the stairs, Connor turned on the light in the attic. It was still filled with furniture, miscellaneous stuff, and boxes. He thought there were lots of nooks and crannies, places where the cats could hide. He peeped in corners and behind boxes. "*Yoo hoo!* Come out wherever you are."

Mary Ann joined him and they looked everywhere. "*Hellooo*...where are you? We know you're here."

They looked everywhere, but they didn't see the cats. Stumped, they came back downstairs. The front door was still open and Tom and Isabella loitered by the entrance as if they had taken a leisurely stroll outside.

"Oh, there you are!" Mary Ann shouted with relief. "You had us worried when we couldn't find you." Apparently the cats had been downstairs and gone out when the door was open. One thing was for sure. The cats weren't fighting; they actually looked friendly. It would be premature to say they were cozy, but they were tolerating each other well. No fights or meowing or any big fuss. That much was good.

"How about a treat before you go?" Connor said as he stretched out his hand with the cat treats in his palm. He waved the treats under Isabella's nose. She sniffed his hand; then she started licking and took the treat. "I think she likes it!"

"Yeah and now that you've spoiled her...she won't like it if I don't give her sweets," pouted May Ann.

"Hey, that's one way to see it. But look at how happy she is," Connor said as he tickled Isabella under the chin. She stretched her neck so he could rub all the way around her neck and down her back. He laughed.

"Meow..." That was Tom. He rubbed Connor's leg to be sure he was going to be noticed. Connor looked down. "Hold on, old man. I've got treats for you, too." He picked the cat up and rubbed his head. "You know I won't forget you. Not ever."

Mary Ann turned to go and waved one hand as she held her cat under the other arm. "I really enjoyed the evening. Bye, thanks for dinner!"

Connor closed the door and leaned against it, still holding Tom. He looked around the home slowly, reliving the moments when the place had returned to being joyful. The words "*home sweet home*" came to mind. Walking toward the kitchen, he grabbed more treats for Tom before he turned the light off.

Chapter 26

Connor woke up to the sound of *pitter-patter* on the roof. This was the first time it had rained since he got home. He stayed in bed, listening to the drops hitting the roof shingles and splashing on the windowpane. When he was a child, he had loved days when it rained. Sometimes there was no school so his friends would come over and hang out. His mother would bake homemade cookies. Ahh...the tantalizing aroma! The minute the kids caught a whiff, they'd make a beeline to the kitchen, especially Mikey and Ron. They had so much fun.

He liked to smell the fresh air when it rained, that indescribable scent. He would suck in as much air as he could, puffing his chest out and filling his lungs. He had always wanted to have a tin roof. Wouldn't that be super cool? Then you would hear the drops splatter and plop on the metal roof. At the moment, Connor was glad that the old roof was solid and built well. No leaks.

Connor's window was slightly open. Tom came into the room and immediately leaped up on the window ledge; he wrinkled his nose at the open window crack, sniffing the rain and feeling the breeze come through the window screen. Connor decided this was a good day to stay home and work on the to-save pile, which was not such a small pile. He was going to take his time with it. He had to focus his thoughts on this home, this place, and what he had come to do. Everything else faded away and seemed like a dream, almost unreal. The reality was in front of him…and Tom, of course. He sank back in bed to watch Tom press his nose into the open window crack. It was almost comical. It was good to be back home.

Everything was still here pretty much as he left it: his toys, his trains, his posters; all his clothes hanging in the closet; his books and papers on the bookshelf; and his collection of toy cars. Each time he came home, it was like he'd never left. He couldn't imagine not being able to come home to his room. That thought frightened him a little. This was the only place he had known growing up. This was where he spent the first eighteen years of his life. He closed his eyes.

He lost track of time. He felt overwhelmed by the memories of his mother and father. The ghosts of his pets flickered by, too. This was depressing, no way around it. He just wanted to lie in bed all day. He felt paralyzed. He had no energy. He rationalized this was a day to stay in bed; he was ahead of schedule, his calendar was clear, and so forth. What was the point of getting up? Why bother? There was nobody, nothing to live for. He didn't want to do anything.

Grief hit him like a sucker punch, right in the soft underbelly where it hurt the most. He lay down on the bed and let the tears flow, wetting the sheets. Then the sobs came out, great heaving sobs and loud wails rising to a crescendo. Tom was no longer at the window. He had leapt away when he heard the wails. It scared him, and he left the room.

Connor didn't care if Tom stayed or left. He opened up his grief, releasing it in the privacy of his home. He could not hold it back. He could not pretend that everything was okay, that he was all right.

He had to feel the grief, to feel the pain of loss, and the void that could never be filled. There were no words to describe it. It was the way it was, the way it had to be. Nothing he could ever do, no matter how hard he tried, could bring her back. He relived his past, his last moments with her. Each time the video ended with his crying, "Mother, Mother come back!" It would rewind and replay, leaving a bigger void. He felt the loss as he curled into a fetal position on his childhood bed in the room that his mother had painted for him after he had childishly demanded that he must have a room painted blue.

Nothing in this world could fix the pain. It was too much to bear. Now in the silence of his room, he faced the pain. All of it. Alone.

Chapter 27

Connor cried himself to sleep, exhausted. Sleep was a blessing. He slept fitfully, deeply, without waking. Outside, the sky turned deep grey; dark clouds gathered, and thunder roared. Still Connor slept.

Connor woke up hours later. The sky had turned black. There were droplets on the window, and the moon hid behind clouds. He finally got up. It occurred to him that he hadn't fed Tom. Poor Tom! He was nowhere in the bedroom. Connor went looking for him and checked his bowls. Tom's water and food bowls were both empty. He brought them to the sink and washed them in soapy water, rinsed them carefully, and dried them. He put fresh water in one. Getting out the bag of cat food, he shook it. No sign of Tom. Again he shook it, louder this time. Tom came darting into the room. Connor filled his bowl and left him to eat in peace.

For once Connor was thankful that the refrigerator was full of leftover food and he didn't have to cook. He pulled out a few containers, dished food onto a plate, piled it high, and heated it. Now would be a good time to drink the wine. Red wine, heavy and robust, aged in wooden barrels. He poured himself a glass and sat down to eat.

He had no idea how hungry he was until he took the first bite. Now his hunger became ravenous, urgent, craving, and needy. He shoveled food in his mouth as fast as he could chew, not bothering to slow down so he could taste the food or feel the texture of each bite. He was not here to enjoy the food; he was just assuaging his hunger as fast as he could. It became mechanical: shove, chew, swallow, shove, chew, swallow. Food was just a means to an end. Filling his body with calories and fuel. Nothing else. He washed it down with gulps of wine. He didn't know and didn't care how much he drank. He used all his energy. When he finished eating, he felt awful. His body was bloated. He put the dishes in the sink, then he walked to the bathroom.

Slowly, he took off all his clothes, layer by layer. Connor stood naked. He stared at himself in the mirror, as if for the first time, as if he were a stranger. He came into the world alone, and would leave the world alone. You couldn't tell someone you wanted to go with them, just like you couldn't tell someone you wanted to be born...or could you? This body, what was it, a bunch of food turned into skin, bones, muscles? It was just flesh. Without nourishment, the flesh would die. How painful would it be for this death to take place? Sometimes people wanted to die.

Sometimes people fought to live, clinging to life as long as they could. In the end, how would he go?

He studied the person in the mirror. The spark inside him, it was still there. He clenched his fist. His eyes blazed as he fought to breathe life back, cell by cell.

Connor stepped into the shower and turned it on full blast, barely feeling the stinging water as it assaulted his skin. He welcomed the hard pinpricks of water. He stood under the shower for a long time, letting the water pummel his hair, his head, and his body. Letting the water wash over him as the rain washed everything outside.

Finally, after a long time, Connor picked up the soap. He soaped his hair, then rinsed it. Then he soaped the rest of his body. He moved over each area, rubbing the soap hard as he moved down his body. It was physical, his fingers touching his skin, gliding over the lather, moving faster and faster, dancing with his fingers over his body. Then he stopped and let the water rinse it all off, watching as the suds gathered at the bottom of the tub, swirling down the drain, until the water became clear.

Chapter 28

Morning came with the bright sun. No sign of clouds or rain. Connor woke to the chirping of birds. Tom was back on his perch on the window sill, paws up and swiping at the birds as if they weren't on the other side of the window. He laughed out loud at how ridiculous Tom looked, swiping away. He got up and swooped Tom off the perch, hugging and kissing him at the same time. "Tom, you old fuddy duddy! Do you know how silly you are swatting at the birds?"

Tom just meowed and jumped down. Seemingly miffed, he led the way to his empty food bowl.

"Aww…is that what you want, Tom?"

Connor filled his bowl with cat food. He watched Tom eat. Tom was a dainty eater, and he licked his bowl clean. Connor made himself a pot of coffee and breakfast before he got down to work. Today he would tackle the huge pile of saved papers. He started pulling out the papers and sorting them into two piles.

The to-save pile and the to-discard pile. He was going to do this as thoroughly as he could.

The day passed quickly. The papers were tedious, but after a while Connor was able to figure out a system and organize them rather quickly. He didn't even have to read most of them; he'd see the header and put it in one pile or the other. He was making good progress with the piles. He was pleased that the to-discard pile was getting bigger than the to-save pile. Trash day was coming up, and he wanted to fill the bins. Tom had padded back to the couch, and it looked like he was going to stay there. *What a life!* Connor couldn't help chuckling to himself. *Tom, you lucky cat.* He wondered if Tom loved him. Do cats know love the way we do? Could Tom love another cat the way we love another human being? Maybe Tom didn't love him; maybe Connor was only a meal ticket to Tom. Well even so, he was going to act as if Tom loved him back. After all, Tom could go anywhere, but he chose to stay here. There were no chains to bind him. Tom always came back. Tom always came home.

The phone rang. "Hello?"

"Hi, Connor. This is your lawyer, Mr. Monroe. How are things going?"

"Hey, Mr. Monroe. I've been going through the things in the house. There's quite a bit of stuff."

"Good. I just want to touch base with you on a few things. Have you thought about what to do with the house? Do you want to sell it?"

"I…I don't know yet. Right now, I'm just concentrating on what I have to do."

"Listen, if you want to sell the house, I know a realtor. I can let her know, and you can talk to her. She may be able to discount her commission."

"Look, I appreciate this. But I can't make a decision now. I need time to think."

"Just call me if you want my help. I'll give her a call if you decide to sell."

"Thanks. I just can't think about this right now." Connor was irritated and upset, and he dropped the handset on the phone. He hadn't given much thought to the house. The decision would not be easy. This was his home. If he sold it, he could never come back to it. There was no hurry. He didn't want to be pressured into selling, even for a reduced commission. The house was paid for, and money was not an issue. He would put aside that decision until all the other stuff was done. He went back to tackle the piles on the floor, hoping to make progress after the unwelcome interruption.

By the end of the day, Connor had gone over all the financial papers. He had even set up online bill-pay for utility bills. His parents were thrifty savers and good money managers. He was not surprised they didn't have any debt. He had picked this up from them. He was careful about his finances and didn't incur debt other than the mortgage on his condo. He knew every month what bills he had to pay and how much money he had left to spend.

There were no messy situations, as some of his friends had experienced when their parents passed. He quickly satisfied the outstanding bills and reconciled the charges. He'd been checking the mail and there wasn't anything unexpected. He put all the paid bills in one pile and the unpaid bills in the other. The thin unpaid stack had utilities bills and a co-pay for a doctor's visit. It would be easy to settle all their financial obligations and move on.

He put old pictures, letters, and cards for birthdays and holidays in the to-save pile. He didn't have the heart to throw them out. His mother had kept them all these years. The people who sent them…some were long gone. Connor felt he was holding a piece of history, a piece that once discarded would remain lost and forgotten forever. This would be a special pile, one that he would go over carefully after he got back to the city. Now was not the time.

Feeling productive, Connor gathered up the discards and put them in trash bags. He took the bags out to the garbage can. He felt like he had put in a full day's work. It was tedious. That's why they called it work; otherwise, it would be called fun. He decided to take a walk. His muscles were tight from being crunched in an awkward position for too long. He wanted to stretch his legs and get some fresh air.

Chapter 29

Connor went back to the house, got his keys and wallet, locked up, and headed for town. Maybe he could pick up something on the way home after he'd worked up a good appetite. He picked up his pace. The stores were still open, but it was getting late. He knew there would still be good light for a while. Connor slowed down to look in the windows, just like he had as a kid when he didn't have much money and all he could do was window shop. Imagine someone coming up with a word for that. Like there was a big difference between shopping inside the store and outside the window. He shrugged.

That was fine when he was a kid; he didn't really give a rat's ass what they called it. The holidays were even better, with bright lights, blinking and sparkly, and the decorations in the windows dazzling and delighting the little boy. But he liked the quietness of the off-seasons too. No Santa or candy canes, but other things. Other interesting things. He was aware that, as sure as the seasons changed, the window dressings changed. He could count on that.

The fanciest building in Rocky Flats was the bank with its marble front exterior. That had to cost a good deal of money. Connor missed some of the stores that had gone out of business in the years since he left town. He recognized some of the family-owned businesses. They had passed from fathers to sons or daughters, aunts, uncles, or cousins. But they managed to stay in the family. Those businesses never changed names. They were the same, with the same signs as he remembered. You wouldn't even know by looking if the father had passed and that it was now owned by another member of the family. It was a smooth transition.

Connor still liked to window shop. He passed each store and tried to remember when he had seen it last. He mused as to whether it had changed owners, or if it was still in the family. Perhaps the new owners preferred to keep the same name so people wouldn't get confused. People were used to old habits; keeping the same name sometimes assured the loyalty of customers. As he walked down Main Street, he passed a mixture of old and new stores. He was rather surprised at the number of new businesses with their fancier storefronts and merchandise from the city. He walked leisurely, with no particular aim in mind, just browsing each storefront as he passed. The only difference from his childhood was that he could now afford to go in and buy items. Reaching the end of one row, he crossed the street and turned around to go back down the other side. It was getting late, and more stores had closed. He quickened his pace to see the last few shops. He didn't have anything in mind that he wanted to buy, so he kept an open mind.

Connor didn't recognize many people on the street, and he doubted they recognized him. A few folks smiled or nodded in passing, just to be polite. He returned the greeting and moved on. If he ran into anyone he knew, he would talk with them. Old men occupied the benches along the sidewalks. Some were socializing; others were waiting for their wives. He wondered if one day he would be waiting for a wife or just be out shooting the breeze with a friend on a lovely afternoon. He wondered if Mrs. Rainer liked to shop and looked for her.

Mary Ann caught sight of him passing the flower shop and looking inside. She waved to him to come in. He quickly walked up the steps and opened the door.

"Hi...saw you waving at me."

"Imagine my surprise. I was just thinking about you...and there you were."

"I'm taking a stroll around town. It's changed since I've been away."

"Well, several new stores have opened since I arrived."

"Do you have suggestions of places to see?"

"Yes, I have a few favorites. The ice cream store next door is one. I wish it wasn't so close sometimes, but it's a favorite of mine. The market is another one.

And…oh, the new restaurant that opened earlier this year has good food. There's also a new bead store where I love to browse. I don't make jewelry, but I've thought about taking lessons to find out if I have any talent."

"I went to the market the other day, but I haven't gone to the others."

"I'm about to close up…would you like me to show you?"

"If you have time, that would be great."

"Hold on, let me close out the register and lock up." She smiled as she went through the routine. In no time at all they were walking out the door. "So where would you like to go first?"

"I was headed this way. I'd like to see the stores on this end and you can show me your favorites."

"Three of them are on this side, the market, the bead store, and the restaurant." She led the way.

Chapter 30

The market was buzzing with people stopping by on their way home to pick up something for dinner. The freshest vegetables and fruits were on display. A small selection of cooked foods showcased the soup of the day, hot entrees, and vegetables. These were made fresh daily.

Connor was impressed by the selection and quality in this small store. He was not happy with the large markets in the city. They threw out so much food every day; it was a huge waste. He figured the amount of food that was thrown out every day could feed an army—a very large army. This market, with its small inventory, maintained tight control, managed the flow, and kept food fresh and waste minimal. Often produce went into the soup or meals instead of being thrown out. The cook got very creative in turning older produce into attractive offerings the next day.

"Hey, Connor," said Mary Ann as she tugged his sleeve lightly. "There's the bead store. Do you want to see that next?"

"Yeah, sure." He could tell that Mary Ann wanted to go in the store. Connor hurried after her. There were rows of containers filled with beads. The variety and colors amazed him. Off to the side were a couple of small rooms with tables. Obviously they were set up for small classes or demonstrations. He saw arrays of jewelry, artfully displayed to show off the beads and designs in finished necklaces, bracelets, and earrings. Mary Ann went straight to the finished pieces, admiring the handiwork and the patterns of beads. She inspected some pieces before she picked out a necklace.

"Isn't this pretty…what do you think?"

He looked at the necklace. The beads were interesting and colorful. He thought the hues matched her dress and eye color, and he told her so.

"I'll take it," she said as she moved toward the register to pay. She immediately took the tag off and put it around her neck, then twirled in delight to show off her necklace.

"It doesn't take much to make you happy," Connor said with a wink.

"I am happy!" she said as she did a curtsy.

They were back on the street in no time and nearing the end of that row. There was one more building at the end, set off a bit from the rest of the stores.

Chapter 31

The sign outside said "Manini's." She tilted her head toward it. "This is the new restaurant I was talking about."

"Do they have good food?"

"Oh, yeah! I like it. The sauces and pasta are made from scratch every day."

"Let's go in. I'd like to try it."

This was the first time Connor had eaten in one of the town's restaurants in many years. Whenever he came home, they always had home-cooked meals. They rarely ate out. This place was new, and it was popular. It was homey and clean. The tables were covered with checkered tablecloths and simple wooden chairs.

The waitress led them to a quiet table in the corner with a view. She took their drink orders and left. Connor scanned his menu and looked up at Mary Ann. "Hmm…what do you recommend?"

"I like the spaghetti and a salad."

"I still have leftover spaghetti at home," said Connor, laughing. "I'll have the spinach lasagna."

The waitress took their orders. The salad arrived in no time. It was chilled, just the way Connor liked it. The entrées came out as they finished their salads.

"I was in the mood for this tonight," Connor said as he cut through thick layers of lasagna packed with spinach and rich cheese filling. He took a bite. "This is delicious. I'm glad you brought me here."

"The food is excellent, and the prices are reasonable," Mary Ann said, nodding as she twirled her spaghetti. "It's a good place to eat."

"So...tell me about yourself. What brought you here?"

"Sure. I had taken a part-time job at a flower shop when I was in college. I got a liberal arts degree with a minor in art. After I graduated, I couldn't find a full-time job. So I continued to work at the flower shop part-time. Along the way, I took some business classes at night. I saw an ad in the paper one day... this store was available for rent. I drove here and took a look at the space. It was small, but it came with a small price tag. I figured I could turn it into a flower shop without spending too much money for renovations. I added some shelves and got new countertops installed. I bought a used refrigerator for the back room, a new display case, and opened up shop."

"I think you still had quite of bit of work to set it up."

"Yes, it took me about a couple of months to get it ready. I got a loan from the bank and placed my first flower order with the distributer and jumped right in." Mary Ann shook her head and looked at him thoughtfully. "If I knew now what I had to do…well, at the time I didn't know better. I thought I'd make a go of it. I didn't have much to lose…small rent, some inventory, and equipment. So why not?"

"How is business now?"

"I have a thriving business. I've built up my clientele. Between holidays, birthdays, anniversaries, and everything else, I'm busy all year. Business has been increasing. Of course there is a spike on holidays, especially Mother's Day and Valentine's Day."

"Are you happy?"

"A part of me says I've been lucky, really lucky. I get to use my creative, artistic side every day, creating floral arrangements. I also get to see my customers and make them happy." She smiled as her eyes lit up. "I'm happy too. Flowers are a big part of celebrations. Everybody likes beautiful flowers. Voila! The best of both worlds." She laughed, raising her arms in a V to emphasize.

"That's a wonderful story. I'm glad you shared it with me."

"So how about you…what's your story?"

"Well, you know I grew up here, you've seen my home." Connor looked at her and paused. "I left here when I was eighteen, right after high school. I went to the big city. I went to community college, then transferred to the state college and graduated with degrees in business and technology. I've been working ever since in the corporate world."

"Uh-huh," Mary Ann prompted.

"I tell myself I'm too busy to come home, except on holidays. The years rolled by, and pretty soon I'd been away for twenty years." He looked at her thoughtfully. "I don't know where my life has gone. I'm thirty-eight. I'm successful in the corporate world, but I don't feel it inside. I feel empty. I don't want to work for another twenty or thirty years to know I'll feel the same way, but with more regret. Regret that I would have spent forty or fifty years in this job and regret at not having lived my life well…and to what end? That I've worked sixty hours or more a week for an impersonal corporation, knowing that I could just as easily be laid off? My life has to mean something more than the corporate profit margin." He sighed. "But then I'm digressing. You asked me a simple question, and I got carried away."

"I want to hear this. I'm interested. I'm thirty-two, and my life isn't perfect either. It may sound perfect to others, but I am not fulfilled."

"I get it."

"I spend a lot of time on my business. I keep the shop open six days a week. I have Sundays off, but I rarely take a whole day off. I have a lot of paperwork, inventory, billing, and all the other non-fun stuff that comes with a business."

"You feel overwhelmed sometimes, with not enough time for yourself…"

"You got that right. I've been doing some calculations, and I can afford to bring on an assistant." She frowned. "I have been thinking about it for a while. When the right person and the right time comes, I'll be able to hand over some of this work."

"Sounds like you have it all planned out," Connor said encouragingly.

"At least for the professional part of my life. The personal part is another story…I can't plan that…" Mary Ann looked pensively out the window. "No matter what I want in my personal life, I can't dictate how and when it's going to happen. One day I'd like a family of my own."

"My mother's passing…my parents' passing. That brought a realization that I'm alone in this world. I'm an only child and always thought I'd have my parents and a home to come back to…" He rubbed his eyes and refocused. "I didn't want this day to come, but the hard reality has set in. I've felt more like a child in the last few days than when I was one," Connor confessed as he gripped his fingers on the edge of the table and pushed away from it, leaning back. "I've got to figure this out…and the rest of my life. I got my wake-up call."

Mary Ann reached out to grab his arm, to reassure him. "Connor, it's not too late. You have time. You do what you want to do…you know what it is, deep inside."

Connor took her hand and squeezed her fingers gently. "I know, but I have to get through this first. I have to…before I can move on."

They lingered over coffee and sat in comfortable silence for a while, each lost in their own thoughts and feelings.

"Hey, Connor! Buddy, how are you?"

"Mikey! Good to see you," said Connor as he looked up to see Mikey at his table. "This is Mary Ann, from the flower shop."

"Hi, Mary Ann," said Mikey. He lowered his voice and turned to Connor. "Man, I'm so sorry about your mom. You doing okay?"

"I'm fine. How about you?"

Mikey turned and gestured to his family watching them from the other table. "I'm married to my high school sweetheart…remember Sally? We have two kids now, boys." Mikey beamed proudly as he waved to them. "You married? Kids?"

"No, not yet. My job at the company, sixty-hour weeks don't leave me much time for anything else," said Connor. He tilted his head toward Sally and the two boys. "You have a beautiful family. I always knew you'd end up with Sally."

"Dang! I'm a lucky guy."

"So what are you doing now for work?"

"I'm still in the plumbing business. My old man passed, and my big brother took over managing the business. Me, I don't like the business end of it so he runs it, and I do the actual work. That's the way I like it. I don't mind getting dirty and crawling under houses." He glanced over at his wife. "But she doesn't like it so much. I tell her a man's got to make a living. She understands."

"I thought you'd end up involved with the family business. You seemed to like it when you helped out your dad."

"Yup, that's what I did. Well, I've got to get back to the family. You holler if you need me, okay?"

"Yeah, thanks man!" Connor shook his hand warmly.

The waitress came back and left the bill.

"You ready to go?" Connor asked as he picked up the bill. Mary Ann tried to grab it, but he wouldn't let her have it. "I've got this."

"Hey, thanks for dinner," she said. "The next one's on me."

"Oh yeah? What makes you think there'll be a next one?" Connor teased, then wished he had kept his mouth shut.

Mary Ann looked away, her cheeks flushed.

Chapter 32

Connor got home later than he expected.

"Tom, where are you?" Connor said, worried when he didn't see Tom in his usual place on the couch. Walking to the kitchen, he ran into Tom sitting next to his empty bowl...waiting. "Hey fella, I'm so sorry I'm late," Connor said as he grabbed the bowl and ran to the sink to wash it.

After Tom ate, Connor rubbed Tom's tummy the way he liked it. Tom purred and stretched and kneaded his paws on Connor's lap in exquisite delight.

Connor viewed the last few piles of to-save boxes and files. He figured just a couple more days would do it. He had labeled some of the boxes, including the one with family pictures, cards, letters, and his school stuff. Others were just papers thrown together. His mother was not the best at filing, and she always had a stack of papers she said she would file when she had a chance, when she could get to it. He worked quickly, promising himself that once this was done, he would reward himself with a treat. He was his own boss. Connor stopped briefly to savor that thought. Hmm!

The next day went quickly. Connor worked steadily, going through everything, tossing things onto a growing to-discard pile. He took a quick break to eat and to brew a fresh pot of coffee. He was high on caffeine, but he needed it to keep going. As he worked, thoughts of the market came to mind, nagging him. He knew about nutritious food and what was healthy. He tried to eat regularly, but that was hard when he was immersed in work. Sometimes at the office he'd binge at lunch to make it through the long workday. If he didn't make it to lunch, he'd binge at the vending machine. He knew it wasn't good for his body. The stuff in the plastic wrappers didn't taste or look fresh. It wasn't like real food.

He made a conscious decision to eat better instead of just grabbing fast food or snacks. All calories were not the same, and Connor's body knew it. It was not too late…he was not middle-aged yet. Uh-oh, how did that slip out? Not that word! Did he really think *middle-aged*? That couldn't be…not yet. That word was not to be used. No, sir. *Cross that word off your list, Connor!*

As he worked, Connor thought of enticing new recipes with fresh green vegetables and the most colorful produce. His imagination ran wild with delicious meals from the cooking channels he watched when he had the time. He loved cooking and experimenting with different foods, textures, flavors. Maybe there was a creative side to him that he didn't know about. As a kid, he had started cooking with his mom. Before he became a teenager, he was preparing meals by himself. His mom wouldn't let him do much cooking on the weekdays when he had school, as she wanted him to focus on his homework and study. She kept it to about one day a week, and that day varied depending on what he had going on...a game, practice or some other activity. However, on the weekends he was free to do the cooking. It might be Saturday dinner or Sunday brunch. He would go shopping with her to get what he needed, but it was basic fare. His parents didn't much care for experimentation. He enjoyed shopping for food almost as much as the cooking. He had a particular fondness for avocados, the feel of an avocado, his fingers running over the rough skin, the firmness of it. When he opened one, he marveled at the size of the seed. How different, how smooth, how round it was! He always wanted to try growing an avocado from the seed.

The thought of food made him hungry. He looked at the clock. It was already seven-thirty. Connor decided to call it quits for the day, pleased with his progress. He heated up the frying pan and made a four-egg omelet with veggies. It was fast, and it took the edge off his hunger. He settled down next to Tom on the couch and turned on the TV.

Over the next day and a half, Connor finished the rest of the sorting. He called the donation truck to pick up one last load of furniture from the attic, and he filled the garbage can with trash. He packed up what was left in boxes and neatly labeled them. It was all that remained of the two people who lived here. But he knew that they had left more, so much more, in the lives they had touched, in the good works they did, and in the generosity of their hearts and their actions. They had lived quietly and didn't make a big show of what they did. But the people who spoke at his mother's funeral paid tribute to her goodness, her works, and how she helped others quietly. The heart-felt words of those people touched him deeply. Each tribute added to the others. Connor closed the last box and taped it up.

Chapter 33

Connor had one more day before his time was up and he had to head back to the city. He used the time to get the house cleaned up. He decided to hold off on the decision to sell the house until after the new year. The holidays would be here in four months.

He got a cat carrier for Tom and loaded up his favorite toys and treats. Tom would have to stay indoors in his condo, and if Connor worked long hours, he would be alone. He worried if Tom would adjust, if he'd be bored in the city, stuck inside a condo all day, all week. Well, they would have to see once they got there, one step at a time.

Connor came across the checklist he had made almost three weeks ago, what he had set out to do. The time had gone by quickly, despite his wish. But he had finished what he came to do.

Finally, Connor needed to say farewell to his mom and dad. It was a short drive to the cemetery. He walked the path to their graves. He said a silent prayer at his mother's freshly dug grave, next to his father's. Connor kneeled, tracing with his finger the area on the lawn where new grass had already sprouted. He moved his hand across the new grass and felt the texture of the soft blades, wishing he could communicate with her, as if the movements could reach her and he could send a message to her. *I miss you, Mom*, he silently mouthed. *I love you so much.*

He closed his eyes and meditated. He heard birds chirping in the trees. Memories flooded back from the time when he was small, the look on her face when she held his hand the first time she took him to school. The look on her face when he brought home his first A. The smile she bestowed when he proudly gave her his homemade Mother's Day card, with his childish scrawling and his drawing of a heart next to a rainbow and a smiley face.

He let his thoughts run free. He felt protective of his mother, even now, and stayed with her for a very long time. He placed the white flowers he had picked up from the market in her flower holder, rearranging them to show their beauty. He placed his hands on his father's plot before he left, shaking loose the slight cramps in his legs from staying in the crouched position.

As he walked back to his car, he turned around one last time.

Chapter 34

Connor felt paws gently digging in his shoulders, waking him. Opening his eyes, he got a close-up look at Tom, inches away. He smiled and reached out to hug him.

"You and me...how do you like that?" Connor bent closer and whispered in his ear. "We are leaving today, my friend." He buried his face in Tom's soft fur and nuzzled him with his nose. Tom gently purred with contentment. Somehow, Tom knew.

Connor went to the kitchen. He got out Tom's favorite cat food and poured it into his bowl. Then he heated up some breakfast burritos and ate quickly. In no time at all, Connor had finished loading his car. He put Tom in his carrier and placed him on the passenger seat.

It was early Sunday morning. There was barely any traffic. Connor made the trip back to the city at a fast clip. Even though it was still afternoon, he encountered some heavy traffic, probably from weekend travelers returning to the city. The familiar highway signs flashed by, between glimpses of tall buildings and landmarks. The dense concrete structures rising from the ground contrasted sharply with the small town Connor had just left behind, nestled in the green valley below rugged mountains.

Tom slept most of the way, thanks to a little pill Connor had gotten from the vet and slipped into Tom's food. It would last until he arrived at his condo. Connor smiled as he checked on Tom again and watched him sleep.

For once Connor was thankful that his condo was a townhouse, and he could park in a garage instead of a high-rise parking deck. He quickly unloaded his stuff and then laid out Tom's bowls with food and fresh water. He gently carried Tom to the couch. The cat stirred slightly in his sleep, but he didn't wake up. Connor used the time to unpack and get settled. He wanted to be there when Tom awoke, to welcome him to his new home. *Yikes*!

Connor brushed away a twinge of guilt at the way he had hijacked Tom away from the surroundings he was used to, wrenching him away from his home. He made a promise that if Tom did not want to stay, he would take him back.

Chapter 35

Sometime in late November

Monday morning came too soon, again. Connor got ready for work, hugging Tom as he left. He backed his car out of the garage and looked back at the townhouse to catch a glimpse of Tom at the living room window, exactly where he was a few minutes earlier. He had not moved an inch.

Connor's thoughts of Tom evaporated during the day, as he dealt with one issue after another. He bought a sandwich and ate it at his desk. The day whizzed by, and before he knew it, people were leaving. Usually he'd stay and work late. But not today.

Connor stopped by the pet store and got food the manager recommended, a more nutritious brand of cat food. He was worried. Tom was losing weight, and he wasn't his usual self.

Tom was there to greet him when he got home. Connor bent down and picked him up, feeling the softness of his fur and the warmth of his little body.

He whispered in his ear, "Tom, fella, I'm glad to see you, too." He breathed a sigh of relief to be home. "I'm so sorry." Connor gently set him down while he washed his bowls and put out the new food. He hoped it would help...but Connor knew it would take more than just food to bring Tom back to his old self.

Connor popped a frozen dinner in the microwave, and minutes later he was having dinner and relaxing on the couch watching the evening news with Tom next to him. He half listened to the dribble on TV. There was nothing newsworthy. At some point he dozed off. He dreamed of the holidays, the town lit up by the decorations, the carolers singing, and snowflakes falling on his face, tickling him...hey! Connor wiped his face to stop the tickling...and woke up to the sight of Tom, his whiskers and fur softly brushing against his skin.

Laughing, Connor grabbed Tom and flicked the tips of his ears affectionately. How he loved the wisps of hair that peered up from his ears.

"Meow!"

"Hey Tom," purred Connor. "How would you like some eggnog? Let's you and I take a trip home for the holidays this December."

Chapter 36

December 23

Connor picked up a bouquet of white flowers before he left the city. The florist put the stems in floral water tubes filled with water to keep them fresh. He cursed under his breath at the late start. Coming home this time, he faced decisions about the house, about Ron's offer, about his and Tom's lives. He hadn't been ready before, four months ago. Going back to the city was what he had to do. It gave him time to think.

With a sigh of relief, he made it to the cemetery before it closed. He glanced at Tom still curled up and asleep in his carrier and smiled. "We're home."

Connor parked at the curb. Stepping out of the car, Connor pulled his coat tighter as a cold gust of wind and snow flurries hit his face. He blew steamy breath out and watched as it lingered, then slowly disappeared. It was quiet, and the hour was getting late. Catching the last rays of the light, he walked quickly up the narrow path to his father and mother's resting place, the bouquet in hand.

Approaching the gravesite, he placed the fresh white flowers in the vase next to her headstone. Connor slipped his hand into his coat pocket and pulled out a sealed envelope. The one with his name on it, written in his mom's familiar handwriting. The one he had found in the box with the cards. He had waited until now to read it, here at her grave. He carefully opened her letter.

Dearest Connor,

If you are reading this then I have passed.

I hope you'll forgive me for not telling you the whole story until now. Many years ago, when I was a young woman, I left to go to the big city. My parents had suddenly passed, and I was alone in this world. I had a boyfriend who adored me. But I thought he wasn't exciting enough and didn't have enough ambition, so I broke up with him. I thought I knew everything.

Once I got to the city, I was able to find a job quickly as a typist. Thanks to my high school typing class, I took the typing test for the job and passed with flying colors. I didn't make much money, but it was enough to live on. I shared an apartment with two other girls in the typist pool. I was giddy with my freedom, my city life. I quickly fell into the wrong crowd. I was naïve...and stupid. I partied with the wrong crowd, didn't know their names. One thing led to another. The rest was a blur. I can't remember the details, but I got pregnant.

I tried to keep working, but I couldn't deal with the morning sickness. I was running out of money and desperate. I finally called my ex-boyfriend back home. It took every bit of courage and I had to swallow my pride. A lot of it. He came immediately to get me. He never spoke of this later. We got married right away. He was a good man, a kind man. I grew to love him, his quiet strength. When I gave birth to you, he was with me at the hospital. Connor, you were the most beautiful baby, the best thing that ever happened to me.

*When you turned 18, I finally told you that your father had adopted you. You took it hard. You were resentful and angry with me, but more so with your father. I am sorry. I hope you'll understand one day and forgive us. He loved you like a father. **More** than a father.*

Love always,
Mom

Connor carefully folded the letter, slid it back inside the envelope, and put it inside his coat pocket. He had avoided coming home, using his work as a convenient excuse. He had lived in a lie for eighteen years and then could not find forgiveness in his heart for the next twenty years. He stood there for a long time in the stillness, seemingly unaware of the snowflakes falling, softly covering his head and clothes and the ground with a delicate layer of white.

Finally, he looked up and glanced at the flowers in her vase. He selected a flower, the one with the longest stem. He turned to the grave beside his mother's and gently placed the daisy over his father's grave.

Chapter 37

December 24

Connor slept well that night…a deep, satisfying sleep. He woke up feeling refreshed, relishing this peaceful moment in his bed, in the familiar blue walls of his old bedroom. Outside, the crisp fresh snow brightened the morning light. Sunlight streamed in the room, bringing with it a new day. He watched Tom sleep, curled up next to him. "Hey lazy bones, it's time to get up," Connor whispered with a smile. He gave him a gentle nudge before swinging his legs over the bed.

Connor dressed quickly in t-shirt and jeans. He filled Tom's bowls with fresh water and food, then dashed out. He drove straight to the flower shop. The place was packed with last-minute customers. He looked for Mary Ann, but he didn't see any sign of her. The woman at the counter ringing up the flower purchases was not her. He maneuvered carefully to the side where it was less crowded to get a closer look, all the while quietly chiding himself for not calling her after he left, even though he needed the time to deal with his own grief. Truthfully, he hadn't been ready to start a relationship then. He had to sort things out first by himself, without adding the complications of a relationship…and not just any relationship, but a long-distance relationship. Connor had seen established relationships break up when separated by distance.

"Excuse me," said Connor as an elderly lady gave him a piercing glance after someone shoved him in her way.

"Young man, mind your manners."

"I'm sorry, ma'am." He flashed her his most charming and sincere smile.

"Well, you should be!"

"May I be of assistance?"

"You can help me move up without being trampled by someone else." She grabbed his elbow and pushed him toward the counter.

"Umm…the lady at the counter…would you happen to know her name?"

"Oh, that's Norma."

"Norma…hmm…is she new?"

"I don't know what you mean by new." She threw him a questioning look. "She's been here for…now let's see, about three, no…almost four months."

"Ah…I see." Connor tried to hide the disappointment in his voice. He did a quick calculation. According to the old woman's timing, that meant Mary Ann left shortly after he did.

"Young man, what are you doing?" she asked as Connor tried to extricate her hand from the crook of his arm.

"I...I think I need to leave."

"You most certainly can't! Not until you've escorted me to the counter."

Connor couldn't come up with another excuse, so he just nodded. By the time it was their turn, the crowd had thinned out. The old lady exchanged a brief pleasantry with Norma. Apparently she had pre-ordered her holiday flowers and she was there to pick them up. Norma looked up her order and pulled out the paperwork. There were some notes written on it.

She searched the flower display case behind the counter. "Let me check on your order," said Norma as she headed toward the rear of the store. "I'll be right back."

He turned around, leaning against the counter while he talked to the old woman as they waited. Connor had a feeling she was a fussy customer and perhaps a bit difficult to please. She was getting irritated, and he sought to calm her down, to avoid a scene if Norma didn't find the flowers she had ordered.

"Connor? Connor...is that you?"

He heard someone call his name, a familiar voice. He turned, coming face to face with Mary Ann standing on the other side of the counter, holding a large holiday vase of flowers. "Mary Ann..." he stammered, confused for a moment, not expecting to see her. He blurted out, "I...I thought you had left."

She shook her head and grinned. "I'm here, Connor. I never left."

"I'm so happy to see you!" shouted Connor.

"I'm glad to see you too," said Mary Ann.

Elated, Connor turned to the somewhat perplexed old woman next to him and gave her a hug. "She's here! I wrongly assumed from what you said about Norma that May Ann had left. Can you believe it?" He paused to catch his breath. "I came here today to see Mary Ann…I left about four months ago. I thought I'd missed my chance when I saw Norma here today."

"I'd put an ad in the paper. Norma answered the ad and became my assistant," said Mary Ann. She set the vase with flowers down on the counter and gestured towards the festive holiday decorations and elegant white lights, strung with long ends hanging down from the ceiling, like falling snowflakes. "This…I couldn't have done this without Norma."

The old woman impatiently grabbed her vase. "Ring me up, will you?" she said to Norma. The old woman turned, looking first at Connor and then at Mary Ann. "You kids should catch up. No time's better than now."

She gave them a wink, then turned to leave.

Please turn this page to read an excerpt of

CHILDREN
OF THE
FUTURE

CHILDREN OF THE FUTURE

Jane Suen

Chapter 1
MONDAY

"I'll see you after school!" Telly shouted above the noise of the engine as he pulled the door closed. Little did he know that today would be different.

He drove the yellow school bus from the small, red brick Rocky Flats Elementary School to the bus yard and parked. He switched vehicles, got in his beat-up blue pickup, and drove to his second job at the cabinet shop.

Stretching his long legs as he swiveled out of his seat, Telly extended the full length of his 6-foot-4 frame until his boots touched the ground. As he turned around and took off his sunglasses, he glimpsed his face in the rear-view mirror as he reached over to put them on the dashboard. Pleased, Telly ran his fingers over his thick sandy hair. His thick head of hair framed a rugged face ... a strong jaw line.

Working in the shop, absorbed in the hum and rhythm of sanding wood, his mind and body were focused and in sync, not missing a beat. Telly quickly lost track of time. Before he knew it, the day had flown by. Telly realized in a panic that he was going to be late picking up the kids at school. He whipped off his safety goggles and dust mask, brushed the sawdust off his t-shirt and jeans, and stomped his boots to shake off the wood shavings. He rushed out, hating to be late. He cursed under his breath. He'd never been late picking up the kids. Telly prided himself for being on time, especially on this job as the bus driver. None of the kids should ever have to wait on him.

He dropped off his truck at the bus yard and drove the bus as fast as he dared. Pulling up in front of the school, he was relieved when he didn't see any kids in the schoolyard. He thought he had made it just in time. But, after he sat and waited, Telly began to think something was out of place. The bell should have rung at 2:30 P.M., and the doors should have opened.

He checked his watch. It seemed to be working fine. It was 2:34 P.M.... but there was still no sign of any kids.

Telly's mind raced, trying to make sense of it. He was not supposed to leave the school bus until all the kids were on it; but, by this time there was no telling how much longer he would have to wait. His eyes searched the school, finally resting on the front door. *To heck with it!* Telly made a quick decision. Grasping the handle, he pushed open the bus door.

As Telly rushed out of his bus to look around, his anger evaporated. A chill filled him, tightening its grip around his heart. He tried to shake it off, but with a sinking feeling, he felt it expand, right down to the pit of his stomach.

The school was strangely quiet, nothing, not a sound. He opened the front door. He heard nothing. There was no sign on the door, and no sign of any kids. Telly went to the principal's office to see if anyone was there. Empty. He peeked in the classrooms. Empty. He walked the halls. The only sound he heard was the *clump-clump* of his boots on the wooden floors. He looked in the schoolyard. Empty. *Where is everyone?*

Chapter 2

FRIDAY, 3 DAYS EARLIER

It was a sunny day. The school bus pulled up and Billy moved forward. The driver opened the door, smiled, and said, "Hey Billy, how's it going?" It was Friday morning and a good start to the day, Telly thought, as he closed the door and drove through the countryside. He stopped the bus a few more times to pick up Ron, Liz, Annie, and Bryan before heading into the small town of Rocky Flats. Telly liked to watch the people buzzing about on their way to wherever they had to go. He wondered where they were going, what they would do with their day. The kids on the bus were chatting and laughing. All in all, just another day like any other, and a beautiful day. He loved his job, all of it.

Pulling up in front of the school, Telly opened the door and said good-bye to the kids as they left. He watched as they disembarked, one by one. The time was 7:50 A.M. Telly stayed there a moment after all the kids were safely off, watching as the last kid disappeared inside Rocky Flats Elementary School. Telly had a second job to go to until it was time to pick up the kids in the afternoon. He drove the bus to the bus yard to make a switch, then drove his truck to his part-time job at the cabinet shop.

"How's it going, Telly?" Ray shouted across the room, as he walked in.

"Hey, man, doing ok!" Telly shouted back as he pulled on his work gloves and got started. The project that he was working on required a bit of concentration and lots of precision. He liked this kind of work, and he was used to it. Some days the rhythm of the work kept him moving at a good pace and the day would pass quickly. He was good at what he did. Always had been. He was good with his hands and good with people. Especially kids. Although Telly didn't have any kids yet, some day … when the right woman came along. But there was plenty of time for that. He was only 27. Tall and slim, he walked with his back straight, almost like a plank. His thick sandy brown hair framed a face already rugged with the vestiges of the outdoors and years of work, honest backbreaking work. On the weekends it was construction, building, yard-work, anything he could get his hands on. Telly loved working outdoors. On a hot day, he often took his shirt off to get a nice tan on his arms and torso. Telly enjoyed the work. It paid the bills and the extra money he picked up now and then went to his savings, for his dream house. Ever since he saw a picture of a tiny house, he had his heart set on one. He wanted to design and build his own tiny house on wheels. And if he did it himself he could save money, but it would take a while … hey who's counting? Telly smiled to himself as he thought about his tiny house, letting the rhythm of his job take over, mingling with the buzz of his sander as he kept it moving in the direction of the wood grain, smoothing the wood, making sure it didn't leave any swirl marks. The day went quickly and soon it was time to pick up the kids.

Telly got into in his reliable old pickup, dropped it at the bus depot, picked up the school bus, and drove a short distance along a well-travelled road he knew so well. It was a familiar routine, like clockwork, where he went every afternoon during the week. He didn't have to wait too long. Promptly at 2:30 P.M. the door opened and the kids rushed out, all at once, talking and laughing. Telly watched as his kids climbed on the bus. He had a good route, a long route that went a few miles out of town. He didn't mind, actually he liked the fact that he had this route. It took him farther out in the countryside, outside of town, and he enjoyed the scenery along the way. It didn't take long to get out of town. Rocky Flats was a small town with a Main Street and stores along both sides of it. Not much more to it than that, but you had most everything you needed.

The kids on Telly's route lived in the countryside. Bryan was the first to get off. He lived with his Dad, a single parent, in a brown house on the right side of the road. He was a cool kid. He liked to be by himself. A little bit of a nerd, you might say, but a good kid nevertheless.

"Hey, Bryan, have a good weekend. See you Monday!"

"Oh yeah, see you," Bryan shouted as he got off the bus.

Telly drove down the road to Annie's house. Annie's Dad was still at work, but Annie's Mom was by the side of the road, as she usually was when he picked Annie up and dropped her off. He knew Annie was a bit embarrassed by her Mom sometimes, but she didn't say that, really. Telly could tell Annie loved her Mom and knew that her Mom loved her too. Telly watched as Annie's Mom gave her a hug and took her lunch bag as they started to walk back to the house. "Bye, Telly," Annie said as she turned to wave. Telly waved back.

Next to leave was Liz. She was ready to go. As always, the minute he opened the door she bounced out, and made a beeline for her house. He barely got the words out, "Bye, Liz, see you Monday," before she disappeared across the yard into her house. Telly watched her to be sure she made it home safely. He knew from talking to Liz that she was a latchkey kid as her parents were still at work.

Just a couple more stops. Ron got up as Telly approached his house. Ron had just had a growth spurt. He was already taller and bigger than the other kids. Ron had a good, easy-going personality and was laid back. He sauntered to the front of the bus and nodded to Telly as his stop came. Telly nodded back, as Ron jumped off the last step and went inside a house with a fence around it, where he lived with his parents and his little sister Darla. Ron had mentioned that although she was only 4-years-old, Darla was already excited about riding the yellow school bus and could hardly wait.

The last stop was Billy's house, a small wood-framed cottage. Billy was wiry and thin, smaller than the other kids. He was smart. But he was not a show-off or stuck-up at all. He lived with his Mom, a single parent. Billy got off the bus and said "Bye, Telly!"

"See you Monday, Billy!"

Telly was done for the day. It was Friday. He was ready for some downtime and a bit of relaxation. It had been a long day since he got up at 6 A.M. After dropping the bus off, he got in his truck and stopped to get a beer at the watering hole. He saw a few folks who had gotten off work already. It's a good place to hang out, he thought as he sat on the barstool. Ray came up and pulled up a stool "Hey, Telly, heard you were looking for another Saturday gig."

"Hi, Ray, you got something for me?"

"Buddy, we could use another pair of hands tomorrow. I'm getting a crew together to install new asphalt roof shingles on old man Caper's house."

"Count me in. What time do you want me there?"

"Six in the morning … we'll get started early and keep going until we're done. Bring your lunch."

Telly smiled. He was pleased to get another day of work outdoors doing what he liked, as he thought about the rhythm of the work and the hammers pounding the nails in. He was concerned about being outdoors as he was already tanned, so sometimes he had to watch it. If he were out too long, he might get a nasty sunburn. He took a swig of beer. That tasted so good going down. After finishing his beer, he got up and paid. Tomorrow was Saturday, and he had to grab a few supplies to get ready for the day.

Chapter 3
SATURDAY, 2 DAYS EARLIER

Telly woke up at 5 A.M. on Saturday, his alarm blaring with radio station chattering. He yawned and stretched his feet over the frame at the end of the bed. It felt great to start the day early. Telly pulled some clean clothes from the laundry basket, since he hadn't had the time to fold and put them away. He pulled on an old T-shirt, a pair of faded jeans, and white work socks. He rummaged in his closet to find the right pair of shoes, the kind that kept him from slipping. He found an old pair of tennis shoes he used for roofing jobs, and he put those on. He also found a large chunk of foam he could sit on while working on the roof, to give him some extra traction and to keep the heat from the asphalt shingles from burning his butt.

Telly made his way to his small kitchen and started the coffee. *Man,* he thought. *There is nothing like a good cup of coffee, dark-roasted and black, just the way he likes it.* He scrambled four eggs in the frying pan and threw in four slabs of bacon at the same time. The kitchen was cozy, with barely enough room for a small table and a couple of chairs. Telly sat down in one of the chairs and ate his breakfast while it was hot. He poured the rest of the coffee in a large travel mug to take with him. He quickly sliced a couple of huge red juicy tomatoes, got some bread out, and slapped them together to make a couple of tomato sandwiches. He pulled on his tool belt, then got into his reliable old blue pickup. It was only 5:40 A.M. He had plenty of time to get there and get situated. A beautiful day; you needed that for a roofing job.

By 6, he met up with Ray and the crew at old man Caper's house. The house was small, and the old man lived alone. The shingle roof had been patched over the years, and it badly needed to be replaced. They quickly got started, taking down the gutters first, then nailing huge sheets of blue tarp over the edge of the house, letting it hang over the side and on top of the lawn. They threw some boards on it to secure the tarp at the ends where it lay flat in the yard. Telly used a flat-head shovel to remove the old shingles and easily popped the rusty nails right off along with the old felt. The blue tarp was a time saver. All he had to do was to toss those old shingles and the old felt over the roof, and they'd fall on the blue tarp and slide down to the ground. Whatever was on the blue tarp would end up in the dumpster.

Roofing was hard and dangerous work. Some guys don't take roofing jobs because of that. A couple of years ago there was an accident, and a guy got hurt real bad. Most of the crew didn't have health insurance, so when they got hurt, each man did what he could to get it taken care of depending on what he could afford to pay. Sometimes you just made do and tried to take care of it yourself. It's the way it goes on these jobs. Telly was not too fond of heights, but he knew that if he thought about it, it only got worse. So Telly tried not to think about it, not to look down, and just concentrated on his job, what he had to do. Soon he was installing new felt, settled into the rhythm of the job, and into the routine. *Bam ... bam ... bam!* The air was filled with the sound of slap tackers stapling the new felt.

The beauty of starting this early was to beat the sun for a few hours. They would work throughout the morning and take a late lunch. Nobody stopped unless you had to pee. Telly kept going, and soon it was time for lunch. He wasn't very hungry but was glad to take a break. Telly ate his tomato sandwiches by his truck where he had parked it in the shade. He wiped his lips with the back of his hand, as he savored the juicy taste with each bite of the thick tomato slices. He didn't want a heavy meal on a job like this. He took swigs from his coffee mug. He had kept it with him, like an extra tool. When he finished, Telly rested a bit in the shade and chatted with the other guys.

Ray was busy making sure they were on track and getting the job done. There was a bonus if they could get it done today. Ray had a good crew with mostly guys he'd worked with before, and they all knew each other. Roofing was not rocket science, but the quality of the work would show through. He didn't want to get called back in the middle of the night or any time when it was raining. Ray knew his job and had planned it out beforehand. There were a few problems he had to work through but no real hitches. He liked working on roofs. It's a specialty that he learned in his early days. This kind of roofing job didn't come too often, but the word had gotten around that he was steady, dependable, and did good work. Folks around here liked that and liked him.

Sometimes Ray tried out a new guy on a job to see how that went, and sometimes it worked out. It wasn't for everyone, though. He had been lucky so far. Actually, common sense had a lot to do with it. He checked people out a bit before he hired them. In a small town, you knew almost everyone. Every now and then someone new came to town, looking for work. Ray prided himself on being able to assess people, and to get a feel for them within a few minutes of having met and talked to them. Today, he had a new man on the crew. A guy had just arrived in town and was looking to make a few bucks. All cash, paid at the end of the day. Ray had talked to him the day before and got the sense he would do an honest day of work and be dependable. The guy's name was Steve. He was scrawny, and he looked like it had been a few days since he had a good shave. When Ray met Steve the day before he had given him an advance which would come out of his pay, so he could get a room and a hot bath. Steve seemed happy to be getting the roofing work today. Ray started him off on some grunt work, but Steve didn't seem to mind. He apparently had solid muscles under his shirt, and he was not a stranger to hard work. Ray looked around and was pleased with this crew today. He had a good crew. It had worked out well.

The work continued at a good clip after lunch. The job was going at such a good pace that the work would be done a bit earlier than expected. They were already putting down new shingles with nail guns. Around suppertime, they finished the job. Ray did a final inspection, and then told the crew to clean up. He got a couple of other guys to come in the evening to pick up all the trash and empty the tarps in the dumpster. It was a good day. Ray was feeling generous, and he told everyone to meet him at the Big Blue Moon Saloon, the favorite bar for working men in Rocky Flats. He was going to buy everyone a beer and give each of them their pay. The crew, including Telly, met there. After Telly got a beer, he sat down and chilled out. He enjoyed the cold beer, taking slow, deep sips.

Life was good. It had been a good week, and Telly had some extra money in his pocket. He had managed his savings well, had watched with satisfaction as it grew, taking him closer to his dream house. His pickup was already paid off. The roomy crew cab was a plus. He didn't mind the scratches and dents; they added character.

Telly got up to go. "Ray, I'm heading out."

"Appreciate your help today, man. Are you going to the cookout tomorrow at John Decker's place?"

"I'm thinking about it," Telly said.

"The whole crew's invited," Ray said. "My sister Jen will be there; she's back in town."

Telly gave him a surprised look. He hadn't seen Jen in years. He remembered seeing her when she was still in pigtails. Last he heard she had gone off to college.

"Okay, Ray, I'll see you at the cookout."